I AM NOT JOEY PIGZA

JACK GANTOS

I AM NOT JOEY PIGZA

SQUARE
FISH

FARRAR STRAUS GIROUX
NEW YORK

For Anne and Mabel

SQUARE
FISH
An Imprint of Macmillan
175 Fifth Avenue
New York, NY 10010
mackids.com

Square Fish books may be purchased for business or promotional use. For information on bulk
purchases, please contact the Macmillan Corporate and Premium Sales Department at
(800) 221-7945 x5442 or by e-mail at specialmarkets@macmillan.com.

Library of Congress Cataloging-in-Publication Data
Gantos, Jack.
I am not Joey Pigza / Jack Gantos.
    p. cm.
Summary: Joey's father returns, calling himself Charles Heinz and apologizing for his
past bad behavior, and he swears that once Joey and his mother change their names and
help him fix up the old diner he has bought, their lives will change for the better.
ISBN 978-1-250-06166-9 (paperback) / ISBN 978-1-4299-3578-4 (e-book)
[1. Attention-deficit hyperactivity disorder—Fiction. 2. Diners (Restaurants)—Fiction.
3. Fathers—Fiction. 4. Lotteries—Fiction. 5. Identity—Fiction.] I. Title.
PZ7.G15334In 2007   [Fic]—dc22   2006038681

The author would like to thank the Boston Athenaeum for its generous support
during the writing of this book.

Originally published in the United States by Farrar Straus Giroux
First Square Fish Edition: 2011
Second Square Fish Edition: 2014
Book designed by Irene Metaxatos
Square Fish logo designed by Filomena Tuosto

7 9 10 8 6

AR: 5.3 / LEXILE: 950L

1

EVERYBODY LOVES A WINNER

You know me. I always have to have something on my mind or something in my hands, otherwise my mind chases off in one direction and my hands go in another. This is how trouble starts for me, because if my mouth controls my mind and my hands control my body then I'm totally split in half and as my grandmother once said to me, "You are like a chicken with its head cut off."

"I am not," I argued right back, puffing out my chest. "My head is *screwed* on!"

"Not for long," she snapped, and lunged at my neck with her bony fingers, but I was too fast and ran off.

Granny didn't like to be wrong, and the next day she brought a live chicken home when Mom was at work and called me out to the backyard. "Watch this!" she said breathlessly as she flicked her cigarette toward St. Mary's Cemetery, which bordered our back-yard. She stepped on the chicken's neck and pressed it to the ground with her bare foot as she raised a hatchet up into the air. "What you see next is just what I'm warning you about."

Then she brought the hatchet down.

"No!" I yelled, and gave her a push from the rear. Suddenly there was blood everywhere and I thought she had chopped her foot off, but it was only the chicken's head. Quickly, she set the headless chicken upright on the dirt and it took off running in circles with blood spurting from its neck until in a spastic moment it flew up and over our side fence and into the unfriendly neighbors' yard and around the far corner of their house. We didn't ever lay eyes on it again.

"See what I mean?" Granny ranted that evening when we smelled roast chicken coming from the neighbors' house while we were eating cold cereal. "When it comes to your head, you either use it or lose it."

That night I slept with my head under the pillow. I didn't want to become someone's dinner, but my sneaky Chihuahua-mix dog, Pablo, dragged that chicken head out of the trash and onto my bed and gnawed on it for his dinner, and when I woke in the morning and saw the pulpy bits of it all ripped apart I threw up, which made a gross thing grosser because he abandoned the chicken head and began to eat my throw-up, which made me throw up again and he wanted to eat that, too. Once, I asked the vet if Pablo could have a med patch like mine to make him less hyper, and the vet said his meds would be called "a cage."

So anyway, today I was walking home from school thinking about this Granny chicken business and wondering if I could make a headless chicken costume for Halloween next week, when I passed a box for a small Little Chef Boy refrigerator and it stopped me in my tracks. As strange as it sounds, refrigerator boxes *really* remind me of my grandmother because in the old days when my spring got wound too tight she was always threatening to put me in a refrigerator and give me a "Special Granny time-out"—which would have been an eternal time-out 'cause everyone knows that if you stick a little kid in a refrigerator for too long then you just have to push the refrigerator over onto its side and it becomes a pretty handy coffin. Just lift the door open so the light pops on, and if it were me inside you'd find my stiff fingers folded neatly around an empty mayonnaise jar and a big creamy white mustache on my upper lip. But it didn't get to this. Granny never could manage to shove me inside a refrigerator because my arms and legs are long and I was like a four-legged octopus gripping the outside edge as she pushed on the soft middle of me.

"I promise to let you out before you turn dark

blue," she'd grunt, huffing and puffing and trying to make a deal. But I knew better, even after she offered me money, because you can't spend it when you are *dead*.

When I saw that box in some neighbor's front yard trash pile I stood there for a minute thinking about Granny, because she is the one who is dead and buried in St. Mary's Cemetery now and I miss her. I didn't mean to start thinking about what she went through—being cremated and her ashes poured into her special jar—but then I did start to imagine it and when I pictured her coffin all in flames and her hair on fire and all the awful thoughts you can have about a dead person you love, I just got really antsy and had to think of something else. I had to *do* something with my hands so I could put my racing mind to rest.

I glanced over my shoulder and made sure nobody was watching, then I hunkered down like a cartoon burglar does before he steals something and I grabbed the box by one of its loose flaps and began to drag it loudly down the street to my house. It sounded like I was dragging a really unhappy animal by the ear. I still wasn't sure what I was going to do with it, but I just had a burning need for that box. I guess I missed my grandmother, and hauling a box around was a lot better than digging up her jar full of ashes for a graveside chat. I knew Mom would flip if I dragged a dirty box off the street in through the front door because of her "house beautiful" rules which just started a few months ago after a big truck pulled up and instantly we had all new furniture and wall-to-wall carpeting.

"Where'd that stuff come from?" I asked her because she was always saying we were flat broke whenever I wanted something new.

"Secret admirer" is all she said, and then she got that lost-in-love look on her face and I dropped the subject. I never like hearing about her boyfriends because *I'm* supposed to be her "big man" around the house.

So I dragged the box around to the back of the house and I guess that's when my mind kicked in because the moment I dropped the box my hands stopped working and I got a big idea. It was so big it allowed me to have fun and do my homework at the same time. When we started studying geography and America's borders this year my teacher, Mr. Turner, pointed to a pull-down map of Canada, and the moment he did I popped up and yelled out that I had been on a bus trip to Niagara Falls with my mom this summer and there was a museum full of the barrels that people used to float down the river and go over the falls in. "And some of those people died!" I shouted. "Died badly!" Before Mr. Turner could warn everyone not to try going over the falls themselves, I added, "And some of the people actually went over the falls with their pets!"

And then when he started speaking again I remembered another detail and shouted out, "And some of the pets died badly, too!"

Not one person in the class believed me. They *never* believed me, because during the Sensitivity Lesson on the first day of school when we were all practicing how to be really honest and kind to each other I was dumb enough to honestly announce that I actually made up more stuff than I really knew because my imagination was bigger than my brain. Since then nobody has believed a word I say, which is not very sensitive of them.

"But this time I'm telling the truth!" I insisted. "At the museum they showed a dog that had been squished on impact and looked like a furry pancake with a tail." I turned left and right and tried my best to look twenty-eight kids in the eyes all at once which only made the center of my eyes vibrate. And while I was in the middle of a shouting match with everyone Mr. Turner stood up and asked us to chill out and then he looked at me and said, "Joey, I want you to do some research on this Niagara Falls subject and get back to us."

Well, when he said "get back to us" I just instantly yelled out, "I'm the king of getting back to you on that!" And he said he knew this already and gave me a wink. I figured some other teachers had warned him that I was sometimes like a windup pirate's parrot screeching *Can I get back to you on that! Can I get back to you on that!*, which used to make me laugh like crazy. I like Mr. Turner because he takes me less seriously than he has to, even though he once asked me if my mouth had a tiny mind all of its own.

I was thinking about all this as I dragged the box up to the top of the slide on my swing set. It was an old kind of slide with a metal surface and not the plastic kind, which is kid-friendly but also kid-boring. I mean, you need something solid and smooth like the metal kind if you are going to coat it with Wesson oil and put a cookie sheet or something on it and fly down. I was going to use the box to experiment with going over the falls. I knew the barrels that people had sat in were filled with some kind of cushioning material, so I raced into the house and yanked some fancy throw pillows off the new couch before Mom saw me. But Pablo and my new dog, Pablita, heard me, which was good because they followed me out back where they could be part of my research experiment.

I shoved one pillow right up into the front of the box and slipped one in on each side, and then I climbed down the ladder and pulled my arms out from my T-shirt holes so that the shirt just hung over my body from the neck down like a poncho. Then I scooped up the dogs and slipped them under my shirt so that their heads stuck out of the empty armholes and made me look like a three-headed freak boy. It was hard to climb the ladder this way so I used my teeth to grip the rungs as I hiked myself up. The metal rungs tasted like rust and dirt and reminded me of the taste of blood, which should have been a warning, but my mind was focused on other things. Once I got to the top I had trouble keeping my balance because the dogs were yapping and scratching up my belly with their jittery sharp nails, but I still managed to crawl into the box and kick out at the top of the ladder with my foot. The three of us went screaming down the falls for half a second before the box slowed down and didn't even drop off the bottom lip of the slide. The whole operation was a Niagara-size dud. And then while my hands were tied up with the dogs my brain really got going, so I imagined that getting the box up on the porch roof might be good because it slants down at an angle and we could really do a daredevil job from there. So I wiggled around until I got us all out and then I got my old plastic wading pool from in the weeds by the back fence. There was rainwater in it and some droopy blow-up toys from summer and I dragged the pool below the porch roof where I thought we would splash down.

It was a great plan.

To make it work I first stuck my head in the back door and listened. I could hear the high-pitched whine and grind of Mom's electric hobby sander. Ever since she had perfected her nail-sculpting skills she'd been telling me that big things were about to happen—like how she might leave the Beauty and the Beast Hair Salon and go into business for herself.

"Mom!" I shouted when she paused the machine. "Can I have a snack?"

"You have to get it yourself," she shouted from upstairs. "I'm styling my toenails."

Perfect, I thought. I grabbed the box and dropped the dogs inside it and then tugged and kicked it across the carpet. Then as quietly as I could I pulled it up the staircase one thump at a time until I had it in the room we didn't often enter because Mom said it was haunted by the smelly "Pigzas of the Past." I knew she meant it was where she had stored some of my dad's junk and his moldy old clothes from when he ran off right before I was born. The room did smell, but I dragged the box across the rough floor and tugged the old wooden window frame up and open and took a deep breath. I looked across the slope of the porch roof. It didn't look steep enough, but then I thought I could put the box in the window with the open end facing me. Then I'd hold a dog in each arm and run from across the far side of the room and dive into the open box which would definitely shoot us across the roof and down.

Then the front doorbell rang. It was the singsongy ding-dong type.

"Can you see who that is?" Mom called out from behind the closed door of her bedroom.

"Do I have to right now?" I yelled back. "It's just some ding-dong."

"Please just do what I ask you to do when I ask you to do it," she yelled back. Then I heard her hair dryer start up and I knew she was now trying to dry the polish on her sculpted toenails as fast as she could. She must have been expecting someone romantic.

"Stay where you are," I said to the dogs, but they didn't and followed me down the stairs then came to a screeching halt right behind my screeching halt as I opened the door.

And there in front of me was my no-good squinty-eyed bad dad, Carter Pigza, who I thought was gone for good last year after he ran off when Mom wouldn't have anything to do with him. I tried to slam the door but he wedged a shiny brown shoe across the threshold. The shoe looked like a gigantic cockroach so I stomped on it. But the bug didn't budge.

"Go away!" I shouted, and stomped on it again.

My dad pushed on the door just enough for his tanned, leathery face to fit through the gap. I pushed back. I wish I could have slammed the door and pinched his head off, but he was too strong for me.

"I know what you are thinking, Joey, but you are wrong," he said, now thrusting his hand in and tapping on the tip of my nose. I jumped back and the door sprang open all the way but he stayed put on the threshold and smiled from one teacup-shaped ear to the other.

"You think I'm your old good-for-nothing dad, Carter Pigza, coming back to cause trouble like before," he started like some wise old owl who could read my mind. "But I'm not Carter Pigza anymore. Nope. You can forget about that Carter guy. He's history!" He puffed himself up. "I'm a new person now. It's like I died and was reincarnated. It's like you've never seen me before. Like you don't know a thing about me—not even my real name. It's like I'm a mystery man to you."

I don't know how he did it but he ran his hand over his weathered face and instantly his deep wrinkles flattened out as if someone had drawn his face on an Etch A Sketch and then gave it a little shake. He looked soft and slightly out of focus.

"I'm a myssssstery man," he hissed, then ran his hand back across his face, which spookily refocused his features.

I stared out at him suspiciously, like I did when the confused person from the retirement home showed up in a trick-or-treat costume in July. Now my dad was dressed differently too—nicer than I'd ever seen him before. Normally he was wearing a greasy work uniform or his scuffed-up old motorcycle leathers, but now he had a suit on with a white shirt and red tie. I glanced down at his shoe, half expecting to see a long shoestring that was a lit fuse, as if this fake Carter Pigza would suddenly blow himself away and the real nutty Carter Pigza would be left standing in front of me snapping at the air like a bad dog on a chain.

"You are scaring me!" I said. "You shouldn't be here! Mom hates you and this is weird."

"Not weird," he countered, raising one finger. "Wonderful! The slate's been wiped clean for me. One day I just woke up and said goodbye to the ugly past and hello to the big bright future. Now I'm a brand-new man with a brand-new plan. I'm Mister Charles Heinz, the man I've always wanted to be."

He was so creepy.

I took a step backward because I was thinking that if he lunged for me I wanted to have a head start.

"And do you know who you are?" he challenged, staring directly into my eyes.

"Yeah," I said calmly. "I'm Joey."

"Not good enough!" he shot back. "You have to dig deeper than just your name to know who you are."

"How deep?"

He thumped himself on his chest with his fist. "To the core!" he said, wide-eyed. "Deep to the core." Suddenly he reached into his pants pocket. I don't know why but I thought he was going to pull out an apple core and give me a demonstration.

I inched back even farther.

"I have a gift for you," he said in a surprisingly different voice. It was a soft, warm voice—the voice I always wished he'd have. Then in a slow and teasing way he tugged out a crisp hundred-dollar bill. "Here, it's all yours," he said, holding it by one corner as a little breeze waved it back and forth.

I leaned way forward until it was in front of my nose then reached up and snapped it out of his fingers. I had never touched a hundred-dollar bill before. I held it up to the light and narrowed my eyes as I searched for the watermark.

"Is it fake?" I asked, turning it over.

"Heck no!" he said, and chuckled at the thought. "And there is plenty more where that comes from." He plucked another hundred from his pocket as easily as pulling a tissue from a box and in one smooth motion he ran it under his nose and gave it a deep, satisfied sniff.

Pablo shuffled forward and gave him a curious look, then sniffed him as if he'd never seen him before.

"Don't you remember this man, Pablo?" I asked, lowering the hundred-dollar bill. "He's the creepy guy who dognapped you last year so he could get Mom's attention."

Pablo just sneezed and drifted toward the living

room with Pablita to watch Spanish soap operas on TV. Mom had been trying to learn Spanish because Lancaster has a lot of Spanish-speaking people now and one came in to get her hair cut and Mom guessed at what she was saying and instead of "trimming the ends" she did something that made her hair look like a feather duster and the woman was so upset Mom vowed to learn Spanish. This made me think of her, so I yelled out, "Mom! I need you. *¡Rápido!*"

I was learning Spanish, too.

"May I come in?" my dad asked calmly.

May I?

He has changed, I thought. He never sounded so polite in all his life. Suddenly I recalled his new name. "Charles Heinz?" I asked. "Where'd you get that?"

"You know, *Heinz*," he repeated, "like the ketchup." He jerked down on his red tie as if he could shake out a few drops. Then he slipped his hand into his inside jacket pocket and removed an ID.

"See," he said, holding it up just out of my reach. It was his face, but with that phony name.

"Does Mom know you changed your name?" I asked.

"Joey," he said, and put his hand over his heart as if I had stabbed him there, "don't be cruel to me. All I've done is to finally discover my true self."

"If you've really changed," I said, "you'll give me that other hundred." I held out my hand. "And I don't take checks or credit cards," I added because he started to look a little shifty.

But I guess he was only distracted because by then Mom was standing behind me. I smelled her before I saw her since she had taken a bubble bath in something called Passion Fruit for Lovers, which was from a party-size free sample we got while visiting the hot-tub showroom the other day. Every time she used it the dogs licked her ankles, even dogs we didn't know.

"*Hola*, Charles," she said in a very formal voice. "Won't you come in, *por favor*?"

I whipped my head around. "Charles?" I repeated. "How do you know his name is Charles?"

She didn't answer that question but reached over my shoulder and gently inched the hundred-dollar bill from Dad's fingers. "Charles and I need to talk for a few minutes," she said in a whispery voice as she slipped the bill up the cuff of her blouse. "Why don't you finish off your snack?" She pointed to the kitchen but she might as well have been pointing to a sign that read TAKE A BACKSEAT now that what's-his-name was here.

"I have research homework to do upstairs," I said, and shoved my cash deep into my pocket before she got that, too.

"Even better," she murmured, and smiled her approval.

Before I turned away I saw Dad point a long finger

toward Mom's outstretched foot. Each of her sculpted toenails peeked out the front of her sandals like a row of red and gold fall leaves.

"Seasonal," he remarked smoothly. "Your artistic talents are impressive." He swooped down and ran a fingertip across her toenails as if they were piano keys.

"Glad you noticed," she replied softly. "Sculpting toenails is a new luxury service only I offer in all of Lancaster. Right now I'm looking for a backer to help me open my own salon."

"What a coincidence," he said, hopping up. "I'm looking to back a good business."

I couldn't listen to any more even if I wanted to. As I passed through the living room I tried to grab the dogs but they sensed something was wrong and darted under the couch. Never mind, I thought, I'll get them for the second run. I pounded up the stairs and went into the storage room. I think my brain was over-worked with trying to make believe that Carter Pigza had not returned and my mother was not calling him Charles because I forgot to use my better judgment and it wasn't until I was running halfway across the room that I thought maybe I should be wearing my bike helmet. Some small part of me heard the dogs yapping from below. I thought they were saying "Think, think, think," but by then I was diving through the air and for a moment I didn't think of anyone—not me, the dogs, or Mom and Dad. What I had planned really worked well because my dive was perfectly aimed and my body was a rocket that went directly through the opening in the box. I slammed into the far closed end of it as if I'd hit the bull's-eye, and the box shot off across the loose roof gravel and I went screaming down over the falls. It was a dark, long drop that became much darker and longer than I expected because I never heard the splash. In fact, I never even hit the wading pool. Instead, I whacked headfirst onto the cement cover over the cesspool.

2
KNOCK OUT PUNCH

I'll tell you this—if you happen to knock yourself out cold by accident and the ambulance has to take you away, then no matter how mad people are that you did something really stupid they will still be happier to see you alive than dead. Sure, later on, after the doctor tells them that your brain has not turned into yogurt from the head-splitting crash, they will give you a long lecture on safety and make you wear a helmet for a while, but in the beginning they are just worried that you might die, or be permanently ruined in some way.

Since I woke up in the hospital I thought maybe the blow on my head had confused me a bit because the first thing I heard after my long scream off the roof was a man weeping as he said, "Wake up, Freddy. Come on, son. Open your eyes. You can do it."

"Yes, sweetie," a woman pleaded. "Wake up, honey."

It was them, Mom and Dad, and as they spoke Dad tapped on the tight gauze bandage that was keeping my skull together and each tap bounced through my brain as if it were on springs.

"I am not Freddy," I moaned with my eyes still closed. "You got me mixed up with another kid. I'm Joey Pigza and my head hurts." I said all of this very softly as if little puffs of white smoke signals were rising out of my mouth.

"You are not Joey Pigza," the man said firmly. "You are now Freddy Heinz, my son. And this is Maria, your mom."

That was news to me. I tilted my face toward them and it hurt so much I thought my head would roll off my shoulders, roll off the bed, roll into a nice dark closet and hide. Instead, I peeked out just a bit and the overhead light stabbed me in the eyes. I must have hurt myself more than I realized and maybe died. I mean, why else would my sobbing new-named parents be staring down at me with their hands clasped together as if they were saying their final prayers over my dead body?

"Did I die?" I asked, and pulled the sheet up over one eye. "Tell me the truth."

"Only your past has died," Dad replied, now smiling as broadly as a game-show host while tugging the sheet down to my chin. "Those dark days are over with. You've just won a great new life as Freddy

Heinz!" He made it sound as if I'd won a prize, a prize so bright and shiny that it made being Joey Pigza seem old and worn out.

Just then a doctor entered the room and leaned over me. "How's the daredevil?" she asked as she reached forward and gently lifted my closed eyelid with her thumb.

I didn't answer, because next she zapped me in the eye with her flashlight and I yelped.

"I think you gave yourself a concussion," she said, then reached down and pinched my toe. "Can you feel this?"

"Ouch," I said. "That hurt."

"Good," she replied. "Now I need to check your mental status by asking you a few quick questions."

"Can I win a prize?" I asked.

"If you get them all right. Now, where are you?" she asked.

"General Hospital," I figured, because it was near our house.

"What day is it?"

"Wednesday."

"What's your name?"

"Joey Pigza!" I said with pride, and squinted over at Dad. He squinted right back and crossed his arms tightly across his body as if he were strapped in a straitjacket.

"I think he's fine," she declared.

I raised my hand. "Where's my prize?" I asked.

"After we take some pictures of your brain and neck and double-check that you are okay, I'll give you copies," she said. "Would you like that?"

I already knew there were brains inside my head. "Can I have ice cream?" I asked. "Then you can take a picture of that inside my stomach."

"We'll see," she said, smiling awkwardly, and left.

The second she was out the door Dad leaned over me. "Freddy," he said. "You gave us quite a scare."

I turned to Mom. "Is this what happens when you die?" I said in my dry, raspy voice. "You become another person, like you get recycled?"

She smiled and ran her hand lightly across my head before reaching for a glass of water. "No, honey, you are still the same nutty kid. Your father and I were just testing out a new name."

I took a sip. "Why should I change my name?" I asked. "There's nothing wrong with it."

Mom glanced over at Dad and gave him an "I told you so" look. "I'll explain more a little later," she said hesitantly, and turned back toward me. "You need a rest."

I did need rest, but now that they got me stirred up I had a few things on my mind.

"What about the dogs?" I asked. That hit on the head made me think they went over the falls with me.

"Charles and I thought it would be fun for you to re-name them later," she added.

"I don't mean that," I said. "I mean, how are they?"

"Oh, they're in the car," she explained.

"Speaking of which," Dad piped in, "they've been in there a long time. I better go take them for a walk."

"Don't dognap them again!" I cried out, trying to sit up, which made me dizzy and I flopped back down.

"Freddy," Dad calmly replied as he leaned low over me and put his hand on my shoulder. "That was the old me who took your dogs. I'm new now, remember? I'm Charles, your good dad, and I'm back. It's time for all of us to forgive and forget the past. I have, so you have nothing in the world to worry about. Now get some rest and I'll see you later—after I walk the dogs and make a few business calls."

He gave Mom a peck on the cheek and whistled a happy tune as he left the room.

Suddenly, I felt my shoulder for my med patch because it needed changing. This much I knew for sure. But it was missing and that made me nervous. "Where are my meds?" I asked anxiously.

"The doctor thought it best to keep you off them un-til she makes sure everything's okay with your noggin. She thinks you had a slight concussion and doesn't want your blood pressure to rise."

"Well, it's giving me a bigger headache just thinking that I don't have my meds. And how can I rest," I asked, "when without my meds I'm restless?" I said *restless* too loudly and my head began to pound.

"*Tranquilo*, little man, *tranquilo*," she said, stroking my forehead. "Now, relax. You might hurt yourself if you get too worked up."

But I was not tranquil. My head still roared like Niagara Falls, and I was worried about not having my meds because Dad took them away the last time he got his hands on me and I didn't trust him no matter what his name was.

I glanced toward the door and sneered. "I'm glad he's gone," I said in a low, cranky voice.

She opened her mouth and a row of hissy little sounds sputtered out as if she were spraying perfume on my words to make them nicer. "Well, since *Charles* is gone," she said, taking a deep breath, "you can just chill out while I get you caught up on a few things."

"Like what?"

"Like your dad and I have been seeing each other again—for a time," she said sheepishly. "For a few months, actually."

It hurt my head to roll my eyes. It was like my brain was doing a somersault. But I couldn't help it. "How could you?" I asked. "After what he did to us."

"But he's changed, Joey, for real," she said with admiration in her voice.

"Only his *name*," I shot right back. "That's like some kind of stupid pet trick."

"It's deeper than that," she insisted. "He's stopped drinking for one thing, and he's sticking to it. He's more of a new man than you think."

"I don't want to think about him," I said, and pouted.

"But you have to," she insisted. "You have to understand how unhappy he has been on the inside. I know he was so crazy before on the outside that you couldn't see what he was like on the inside, but if you did you'd see a very unhappy person. That's the Carter Pigza I remember—the unhappy one, and every crazy thing he did was because he was so sad and confused with himself and who he is. And it's up to us to see this and try to help him like his new self better."

She must have seen the suspicious look on my face that said I was having a hard time believing not only what she was saying, but that there was some invisible goodness deep inside of Carter Pigza I hadn't seen. Then she turned on me in a way that was so nice but so painful at the same time.

"You know, Joey," she said in a quiet voice as she reached for my hand and gently held it, "when you were having all your troubles behaving in school, it was other people who looked into your heart and saw that you were a good kid. That you were not just that out-of-control wild kid on the outside, but the real sweet kid was on the inside, deep down inside where hardly anyone could see, and only the people who truly loved you could see it, and they took the time to see the goodness in you and it changed your whole life. You know this is true, and now Carter—I mean, Charles—needs your help to show him that it's okay to be the best part of himself."

"Why is it up to me to save him?" I pleaded, and I could barely ask the question because after what all she said I felt a fearful weight crushing down on what was left of my little body. "Why me?" I whimpered.

"Because you have been very unhappy in the past," she said, "and now you are not, so you know what it is like to change."

I felt tired just trying to imagine where that goodness might be in my dad. And I felt that trying to find it was going to be like crawling down one of those old dark coal mines around here that were gated shut because they were dangerous. He once pointed one out to me and said, "A man would make a million dollars if he could find a way to turn coal into diamonds." And now I was being asked by Mom to unlock one of those gates and feel my way down that cold shaft and somehow, some way I couldn't even guess at, find a way to turn his coal-black heart into a diamond. But if no one else had ever figured out how to do it, I didn't think I could either.

"Is this what you are asking me to do?" I asked after I pulled myself together and told her about the mine shaft being like Dad.

"Yes," she said brightly. "That's it exactly. His heart is a diamond in the rough and you can help me find a way to polish him up."

The way she said "diamond in the rough" made me think of some old country-and-western song, and I wondered if this was where she got the whole idea of his "goodness way down deep inside." But I guess it didn't matter where she got the idea as long as she believed in it. And maybe that was the same with Dad—it wasn't about what was true, or what was real, it was about what he believed. And Carter Pigza *believed* he was Charles Heinz.

"You forgave me," she continued, and held my hands in hers. "You forgave yourself. You even forgave your crazy granny. Now it's Carter's turn. Like he said, you have to forgive and forget, and I challenge you to find the goodness deep inside your father," she said. "I know it's there, Joey—all he wants is a second chance to be a *número uno* dad."

This was going to be a big job, bigger than my bruised head could imagine.

"But I don't understand, Mom. How could you forgive him after all the bad stuff he's done to you?"

"For better or for worse," she recited. "Those were the words I promised God when we were married. And"—she paused and sat up straight and stuck her chin out as if what she was about to say was going to cause a riot—"we are actually still married."

"Married!" I cried out. "I thought you divorced him a long time ago."

"I chased him off," she explained, "but I never had the extra cash to *actually* get the divorce."

"I have a hundred bucks," I offered. "Will that help?"

She didn't answer me. Instead, she quickly jumped tracks and switched the conversation in another direction.

"There is another thing I didn't tell you," she chirped, suddenly full of joy. "Charles has won the lottery—not a lot, but enough to give us a fresh start, and he has some good ideas on how we can improve our family life."

"Won the lottery?" I said doubtfully. "I'll believe it when I see it 'cause he might have made that up, too."

"It's real, Joey," she said, "because ever since your dad won all that money he's been so helpful. I mean, where do you think we got the new furniture and carpeting? He's finally learning to be a man and look after us." She looked so lovesick I thought she should crawl into the hospital bed with me. "He's become a new man," she whispered.

"He's certainly different," I remarked. "So different he thinks he is someone else."

"It's more than that," she went on. "The money has settled him down. Allowed him to make plans and follow through on his dreams. And now that he has the money to make his dreams come true . . . well"—she hesitated and gave me her big-eyed-doll look—"I've always been one of his sweet dreams, so now he can make me come true. After all, our wedding vows *did* say 'for richer or for poorer' and now that he's richer we can say goodbye to poorer."

At the moment it seemed the money had changed her more than it had changed him. He had always wanted to be with her, but she didn't want anything to do with him. Until he won the lottery. Now it all made sense that she was happy he was back. And even though I loved her so much I still wanted to say, *Aren't you just after him for the money? Isn't that goodness deep down inside him located in his wallet?*

Suddenly, I snapped my fingers. "Now I understand about the money," I said.

"What?" she asked.

"Back at the house he gave me a hundred bucks. And I'll bet you my hundred that he's just walked out of here and is gone for good." I pointed toward the hospital room door. "The moment anything goes wrong he runs away, and now that I'm hurt I bet he's changed his name to the Jolly Green Giant and has headed for the hills." I knew my voice sounded mean, but I wanted to hurt her for now liking him.

"Well," she said slowly, "I'll take you up on that little ol' bet. He cried like a baby after we heard the crash and found you knocked out cold in that box. I know he loves you just as I know he loves me and that he's back to stay."

"We'll see," I said. "Shake on it."

I stuck out my hand and she gave it a shake. Then she stood up and looked closely at her face in the mirror.

"I've been thinking about the silver lining to your accident," she said. "I think there's a gift in it somewhere."

Before I could ask about what the gift might be Dad shuffled through the door singing, "I'm a happy dreamer, I believe love can change the world." I stared at him as though a ghost had returned because I really did think he had run off, but here he was dancing back into my life as a happy dreamer, which seemed more like a scary nightmare.

He smiled at me with that goofy wide grin of his. "I picked you a bouquet of joy," he sang in his cheerful voice, and like a magician he pulled a bunch of faded yellow mums from around his back. "The nurse put them in a paper cup for me." He set the flowers down on my bedside table. I took a sniff and pulled my nose back.

"Did you pick these in the smoking section outside the front door?" I asked.

"As a matter of fact, I did," he admitted proudly. "They have a little garden out there and I didn't want them to go to waste now that the weather is turning."

I thought the smoky blossoms might start coughing and wilt like my grandmother, who turned the color of beef jerky as she smoked herself to death.

"Feeling better?" he asked, and nicked me on the chin with a fake punch.

I jerked my head back. "Different," I replied.

"Well, that's the first step toward positive change," he said with enthusiasm. "Yes, sir," he said firmly, "there is nothing like feeling different from yourself to know you are on the mend." Then he turned to Mom. "By the way, the nurse said visiting hours are about over. They are going to wheel Freddy to radiology and then they need to keep him overnight for observation. Why don't we let him get some rest and I'll take you out for a *special* dinner."

"Okay with you, wild thing?" Mom asked me.

I nodded okay back because if I had said yes I wouldn't have meant it.

She bent down to kiss me and then buzzed my ear with her lips. "I'll give you a second chance on that bet," she whispered, "if you give him a second chance."

She pulled away so she could look me in the eyes.

I had never had a hundred dollars before and hated to lose it so quickly. "Okay," I said reluctantly. I figured it didn't cost anything to give him a second chance because he was sure to blow it.

After Dad left to get his car, the doctor came in and

talked Mom and me through what was going to happen that night, and then Mom gathered her things and got ready to go. I was actually glad to be spending the night away from her because she was acting so nutty.

She gave me another kiss, then walked quickly toward the door. "See you in the morning, *chico*," she said before slipping out of sight.

"Hey, what's my silver-lining gift?" I called behind her before she was out of earshot.

A moment later she stuck her head back in. "Forgiving him is going to be the greatest gift you ever gave yourself," she said, then quickly ducked out.

It wasn't until after she'd been gone for a few minutes I realized I'd been laughing as if what she said was the funniest joke ever, but it wasn't funny. Still, her punch line kept me laughing while my hands covered up my big bandaged head until finally I just couldn't laugh any longer and I dropped back onto the pillow like a knocked-out boxer. "Forgive him?" I moaned. "How?"

I couldn't answer because my head began to throb and my brain swelled up like a sponge full of tears.

3

HANDCUFFED HEARTS

Over the next few weeks there were a string of surprises that went off one by one like a pack of firecrackers. The first bang let loose the next day when I got home from the hospital. My head felt woozy and my legs were shaking as I walked up the front porch steps and into the living room while trying not to step on the dogs, who were chewing on my hospital booties that I wanted to keep as souvenirs. I plopped onto the couch and that's when Mom stooped down and looked at me from about six inches away from my face. Then she moved closer and closer until our noses touched and I felt like a cross-eyed frog.

"What?" I asked, pulling back and looking from her to my dad. "What's going on? Why are you being so *loco*?"

Suddenly she shrieked, "Last night your father asked me to remarry him!"

The force of her scream blew me back against the couch cushion.

She jumped up and down and did a little happy hamster dance, which made my head throb even more. I was stunned. *Remarry?* She might just as well have told me Charles was actually an alien that inhabited Carter's body.

"I thought you already were married," I said, and breathed deeply to keep myself calm.

"We're having a renewal-of-vows ceremony," Mom answered. She looked at Dad and smiled sweetly.

He grinned like a carved pumpkin, and a warm light glowed from his eyes and mouth. "I love her," he crooned. "She's my dream angel from heaven and I can't do without her."

"We'll be a whole family again," Mom continued. "*¡Una familia perfecta!*"

"And a church blessing will mean we aren't just living together in *sin*," Dad explained, as he rested his arm around Mom's waist.

He said *sin* like it was something he had always avoided.

Mom's face got all soft as she tilted her cheek onto his shoulder. "A dream angel is a delicate creature that can only survive in heaven on earth," she purred.

I thought the only way to survive this surprise was to give up my meds and just go crazy on my own before they dragged me into their insane world.

But I guess even the sane get used to living with the insane, which kind of turned my world upside down. I stayed home instead of going to school, and passed out candy on Halloween instead of going trick-or-treating, and instead of being Mom's "big man of the house" I went back to being her "little man," which was like getting kicked all the way back into second place, which around here is like last place, which is where I spent most of my life, and so I didn't like it at all, especially since I had worked so hard to be my *own man* in the first place. In no time at all my world was replaced by their new made-up world of heavenly love and before long I found myself at the church on the day of what they called the rewedding.

They insisted I be the ring bearer, which made me nervous, and to make matters worse my mind was a bit drifty since I wasn't allowed to take my meds because of my headaches. I warned them about this but they didn't listen. So on the big day I slowly walked up the church aisle while some guy with a karaoke machine at the back of the room sang, "My love must be a kind of blind love," and even though I thought love must definitely be blind because Mom was acting like a different person and Dad was using a fake name, I kept focusing down on the little heart-shaped pillow and the two gold rings which were my responsibility to deliver to the front of the church. My arms were shaking and the little rings, side by side, looked like a tiny pair of vibrating handcuffs. I didn't dare look away much from the rings for fear of dropping them.

To my left were a dozen of Mom's lady friends from the hair salon who all had their hair done up like fancy pastries and elaborate birdcages. To the right my dad's friends from who-knows-where kept looking at their watches and shifting anxiously in their seats. I was in a silky white rented tuxedo over a white shirt that had fluffy ruffles from my belly button up to my chin. It looked like someone had sprayed my chest with canned whipped cream and topped it all off with a giant pink satin butterfly bow tie. For safety reasons Mom and Dad said I had to wear an adult-size bicycle helmet over the bandage around my hurt head. Dad had sprayed the helmet white to match my outfit and Mom had put little heart stickers and cupids around the edge. But the thought of that helmet hurt worse than the blow I took to my head.

I was too old for this job. I told them so, but Mom insisted that it was the perfect activity for her "little angel." If anything I wanted to be the best man, but my dad had one of his buddies stand by his side. He had met a lot of really nice but troubled people at Alcoholics Anonymous, and this guy, Dick, who was built like a bloated bowling pin covered with see-through hair that stood out the same as on a plastic bottle brush, was now his new best friend. They had worked together as roofers in Pittsburgh before moving their business back to Lancaster. I don't know how Dick got on a roof, because he looked so big in the belly he couldn't tie his own shoes and only wore bedroom slippers. They called themselves DEATH-WISH ROOFERS, Dad told me, because they would climb up onto any roof no matter how tall or steeply pitched. I guess their "death wish" created a bond between them, which means you could call Mom and Dad getting re-married a sequel to the "Until death do you part" wish. Dad said to me that he and I already had a bond so there was no need to build one, but our bond was still just on my "wish list" and not yet on my "wishes ful-filled" list. I knew forgiveness would definitely be good for him, but maybe because I had been in the hospital with a busted head I just wasn't strong enough yet to forgive him.

Before the rewedding had started, Dad and I were down in the church basement getting dressed. There was a life-size Christmas manger scene stored there with the three kings and Mary and Joseph, and Dad had his foot propped up on the cradle next to baby Je-sus' head and was tying his big shoe.

"You know, Freddy," he said to me, "one day when I was up on some roof sweatin' and cursin' myself for being such a loser, it just came to me out of nowhere—

like a voice from a low-flying plane—that I should go buy a lottery ticket and then wait for my life to transform into something better. So I did what my thoughts told me to do. I tied my end of the safety rope around a chimney so Dick wouldn't fall off the roof and I hustled down to the street and walked over to a convenience store. Right up front was a huge display of ketchup and it just popped into my head that I was Mister Charles Heinz, and then I swaggered up to the counter where the nice man from India asked, 'What can I do for you?' and I replied, 'I want a lottery ticket.' The dates for your birthday and your mother's birthday just popped into my head, and I gave the man those numbers and one other number and he gave me the lottery ticket. Soon as I touched it I knew it was a winner. I went home and took a shower 'cause I figured the newspaper would want to take a picture of me. I started right then and there to pack my belongings. Anything that said Carter Pigza on it I threw away. When Dick came home after yelling down to the street and begging people to haul him up the rope I told him about what happened and he laughed at me, which was okay 'cause he probably should have been mad with the way I left him hanging. Then we watched the lottery after dinner and the lady called out the numbers and right away it was your birthday and year, then your mom's, and then there was that one more number I picked. I had used Carter's lucky number and that was the one number I missed. I should have used Charles's lucky number, but I didn't think of it. Dang! As a result I didn't win the ten-million-dollar mega jackpot, but I did win a nice chunk of change. I guess fate thought if I won the big one I'd go just hog wild like a hot air balloon with a hole in it until I crashed and burned."

He rubbed his chin and nodded reflectively. He began to tie his other shoe before starting up again.

"No, fate was smart. Gave me just enough cash to force me to make sensible decisions. And here I am now," he said matter-of-factly. "The complete package. Man. Dad. Happy dreamer and soon to be a re-husband all over again."

"Do you really think you heard a voice from a low-flying plane?" I asked him. I couldn't get over that.

He didn't answer, because just then his foot slipped off the cradle and he fell forward with a holler, ripped open the back seam of his tuxedo, and knocked over the three kings. Two of them had gold crowns on and when the statues hit the floor the crowns rolled away.

That should have been an omen to me about the rings I was now carrying as I took baby steps up the aisle while holding the pillow in both hands. I had to concentrate and make sure I kept the pillow balanced just right. When I got closer I glanced up and could see that Mom had given herself a tight-curled perm and a spaghetti-sauce-red dye job. It wasn't what I expected when she said she was planning a new hairdo to wipe the slate clean and have a fresh start with "Charles." Really, when she said that I thought the hair dye and dryer heat over the years had softened her brain because it was like asking for a fresh start with someone who was rotten to the core.

"He's nuts!" I had said to Mom after she told me about the renewal ceremony. "His name is *Carter*. Remember!"

"Well, I think we should respect his wishes to be called Charles," she said firmly.

"That's insane," I pleaded. "It is not like calling someone Bob when their name is Robert, or Matt when it's Matthew. He has totally flipped out and is calling himself some other name because he thinks he has become someone else. It's like Pablo thinking he is a Great Dane."

"Well, you know," she said thoughtfully, "that identity change has done him the world of good, and it would be good for us, too. Just think, overnight you can become a whole new person and toss into the trash can all the junk from your past. And becoming Maria has already done me some good, too. Every time I remember something stupid I did as Fran, I just give my head a shake and say, 'That's not me anymore.' And the memory vanishes like magic, like pouring bleach on a stain."

"Please don't do this," I begged. I wanted to beat my

head against the wall but at the time I didn't have my helmet on.

Mom ignored me. "Adults behave in ways kids can't yet understand. When you grow up and have a kid you'll see what I mean. You'll understand then that your father and I share a bond between us that can never be broken. We messed up a few times but now we have a chance to pull ourselves together, and as adults you don't get a second chance very often. Can you understand that?"

"But what if your second chance ruins my first chance?" I argued.

"I'm the adult," she said impatiently. "Ultimately what's good for me is good for you. Anyway, you should feel lucky that your father and I are getting back together. I'm doing this for you."

I didn't feel lucky, really. Besides, I thought if growing up means that you just make the same dumb mistakes over and over, then I don't want any part of "seeing what she means." Before I got my meds and some help I used to make the same mistakes over and over and it led to nothing but trouble. My old teacher down at the Special Ed Center, Mr. Special Ed, said that not learning from my mistakes would always lead me to trouble. This was one of his Rules of Life. But maybe Mom's "second chance" thing was just too much for me to understand.

To keep from flipping out as I walked up the aisle, I

tried to think of something good to help me calm down. I lowered my eyes and looked at the two rings and I thought of my two dogs, Pablo and Pablita. Mom said I should rename them to fit our new family, so I began thinking of new Heinz family names for them. I thought about Salt and Pepper, Ketchup and Mustard, Sweet and Sour, Paper and Plastic, Nacho and Cheese, but I didn't know enough Spanish to know if they would sound good when translated.

Then disaster struck, but it wasn't all my fault. Mom didn't take me to rent my tuxedo until the last minute, because she made me stay in bed while my busted head could heal. She stayed in bed a lot, too, with the flu or something, and Dad was out "taking care of business" most days. I had told Mom my head felt fine but I think she was just trying to keep me out of the way while she dreamed up their crazy rewedding ceremony. Anyway, the only pants that fit me in the waist were too long in the legs, so Mom had used a bunch of Scotch tape to hem them on the inside, and I knew that the tape was a weak link, which is why I steadied my hands around that pillow as I shuffled my feet forward. I didn't want to walk normally, because I was afraid of stepping on a pant leg if the hem came undone.

But as I made it halfway up the aisle I was confronted by a pretty big test. Right across the center of the aisle there was a little pyramid of steps—three up to a little platform, and three down. Some wedding-planner girlfriend had put this idea together so that Mom and Dad could each climb up the little pyramid and pause at the top to turn and wave to everyone— which they had done, and it was a big hit with the crowd. And now it was my turn to climb up and tilt the pillow forward for everyone to see the rings as I displayed them to my left and then to my right. Then I was supposed to climb down, shuffle up to the altar and be ready to offer them to the reverend when he requested them. No one in the history of wedding planning had ever heard of such a ring-showing-off ceremony, which is why my revamped parents did it. They love to be the first to do anything which I call "weird" and they call "unique." It was like one of those nutty creative-name ideas Mom came up with once in a while. She suggested I "personalize" my name and change the spelling from Joey to JO-E.

"NO-E!" I said to her. "I like my name spelled how it is."

"I'll get you a gold chain with a big JO-E spelled out in diamonds," she said. "It will look stunning around your neck."

"Diamonds?" I questioned.

"I mean diamond-like," she said, waving off my critical look.

"I'm going to stay Joey," I said. "I don't want to be *Joey-like*."

Later, she tried again with Freddy. "Why don't you spell it P-h-r-e-d-i," she suggested. "Give it a distinctive *flair*."

"You really don't want me to go through life like that," I asked, "do you?"

Mom let it go, but when it came to the rewedding, she was geared up to try everything nobody had dared do before. She had to "personalize" everything. First I was to climb the pyramid and reveal the rings like a waiter showing off a tray of fancy desserts. Then there was going to be the wedding ceremony with vows of undying love they wrote themselves. Then gold and black balloons were going to drop from a net under the ceiling of the rental church—each balloon had QUIPS PUB and GO STEELERS! printed on it because they were donated by the sports bar where the reception was taking place. Then outside were a few cages of pigeons—Charles paid some buddies to catch them with butterfly nets. They would be released as Mom and Dad did some sort of Broadway tango down the church steps toward their rented white Hummer limousine, which was as long and wide as a house trailer.

I was thinking about all of this and not fully paying attention to what I was doing, which was a mistake on my part. I got up to the top of the pyramid okay and leaned forward a bit and tilted the pillow but not so much that the rings could slide off. I turned left, then right, and the crowd oohed and aahed, and then I began to step down and that's when the Scotch-taped hem let loose and I caught my other foot on it and fell forward with the pillow held out in front of me as I belly flopped into the aisle. The crowd gasped and the rings bounced into the air and rolled away under the pews, where they curled around and around in circles far from me. I couldn't move because the wind was knocked clear out of my lungs and my head rang like a gong.

Unfortunately, the ceremony was only delayed for a few moments. The rings were quickly found and two men hoisted me back up onto my feet and the pillow was thrust back into my hands and the rings placed on the pillow while some thoughtful lady rolled up my pant legs, then the music picked up where it left off and I limped forward as if I were going to stand before a firing squad where I was delivering by pillow the very bullets that would soon kill me. At that moment I wished I were dead. It didn't help that when I made it to the altar Dad glanced down at me and whispered, "You are a chip off the old block."

And then the reverend cleared his throat and turned to the audience with upturned arms. "Welcome, friends," he announced with a wide smile on his face. "Please rise."

Everyone stood and stared at us.

"Forgiveness," the reverend continued while reading from a sheet of paper, "and the rebirth of romance

and love are the chosen themes of this glorious renewal. So let us all witness this heartfelt ceremony
that melts away blame and enmity as Carter and Fran
Pigza embrace their new lives as Charles and Maria
Heinz. Let us all forgive and forget the past and give
praise to the never-ending healing power of true love."

I looked over at Mom just in time to see her pull a
small piece of paper out of her bouquet of flowers. She
glanced at it and stepped forward. "Charles Heinz,"
she said nervously, "in front of my friends and family I
want to forgive you for all the hurtful things you have
said and done to me as Carter Pigza."

"And I," Dad said in a loud voice as he stepped forward, "want to forgive you, Maria Heinz, for all the
hurtful things you have said and done to me as Fran
Pigza."

Then Mom took a deep breath and spoke. "I forgive
you for leaving me when I was pregnant with our son,
Freddy."

Suddenly all of Mom's lady friends squeezed together like a chorus and sang out, "She forgives!"

Then Dad announced, "I forgive you for all the
times you called me a lifelong loser."

Dad's friends cried out, "He forgives!"

Mom followed with, "I forgive you for trying to run
me over with your motorcycle last year."

"She forgives!" sang Mom's chorus.

"And I," Dad said, "forgive you for throwing my

signed Roberto Clemente ball at my face and nearly blinding me."

"He forgives!" the men declared.

Mom forgave him for stealing my dogs, flushing my meds down the toilet, pulling his mother out of her own coffin, and much, much more. He forgave her for threatening him with an electric knife, setting his clothes on fire, and stealing money from his wallet when he was drunk.

The two choruses of friends went back and forth as the lists of things they each forgave grew longer and longer. My mouth must have dropped open and stayed open for the entire ceremony as I gaped back and forth and listened to each new unkindness that needed forgiving.

At one point Dad hesitated and I thought he had finally run out of things to say, but then Dick leaned forward and whispered in his ear and Dad suddenly shouted at Mom as he pointed at her, "Oh, I forgive you for making me quit drinking."

"He forgives!" Dad's choir sang out.

It was at that moment I thought the accusations were overpowering the forgiveness and wondered if listing all these awful things they did to each other might be stirring up too many bad memories.

But before Mom could add another horrid incident to her list, the reverend wisely stepped forward and loudly said, "The rings, please!"

I nearly forgot I had them, and as I raised the pillow he snatched them up and hurriedly put one on Mom and one on Dad then turned to the audience and said, "I now give you the renewed and renamed Maria and Charles Heinz, and son Freddy."

The audience clapped and the balloons somehow got stuck in the net, so Dick climbed up onto the altar with the long-handled offering basket and swung wildly at the net until he ripped it open and the balloons drifted down and my parents marched out to the song "We Are the Champions," and then as they exited the church the pigeons were let loose and a couple people had to wipe nasty white splotches of pigeon poop off their heads and shoulders. It was a sight that got me laughing really hard, and at that moment I realized another surprise—*I* was having fun despite myself. After I realized this I began to think the entire ceremony was so cool, especially when they danced down the steps and Mom smiled her great big giddy smile. If this was what made her happy then it was good enough to make me happy, too. I waved at her with both my arms overhead and she winked back at me and blew me a kiss. Then on the sidewalk she turned and threw the bouquet over her shoulder and instantly there was a huge scuffle of wild-haired women on their hands and knees as Maria and Charles Heinz hopped up and into their Hummer limo, which zoomed off with about ten thousand crushed diet soda cans tied to the back bumper along with a few loaves of white bread.

"Come on, Freddy!" Dick hollered from his pickup truck. "I'm taking you to the reception!"

"I'm Joey," I said.

"Whatever. Just get in the truck," he ordered.

I pulled up my pants and ran down the steps and into his front seat and slammed the door shut. He mashed down on the gas and I was glad I had my helmet on as my head snapped back and hit his gun rack.

"Some rewedding, huh?" he asked, and took a swig from a whiskey bottle. "Want some? 'Cause it's a booze-free zone for me when I get there. I'm not allowed to drink in public."

I passed, and he finished the bottle and flipped it out the window and into the back of the truck.

"The rewedding was great," I said because I was thinking of Mom's smile, which was so wide and so big it kept me from thinking about all the negative thoughts I had. It was a magical smile and I was definitely under her spell. Of course I understood that her smile was the result of the two of them redoing their wedding vows, so I had to think that he did her some good. But was that the same as there being some good way down deep inside of him? I didn't know for sure, but I hoped so because only time would tell.

At the reception I watched as they danced, and he

danced so smoothly, as if he really were some rich guy named Charles Heinz. And then he stood on a chair and gave an amazing speech about how Mom was the greatest woman in the world, with the most forgiving heart and the most angelic face, and that he was the luckiest man on the planet. When it was her turn to speak she said that she never would have guessed she'd marry the same man twice, but she figured that the second time around was the ticket to lifelong happiness and that if you couldn't forgive a person for changing for the better then you didn't deserve to be forgiven for your own mess-ups because "It takes two to tangle."

Everyone clapped and whistled and raised their glasses for a ginger-ale toast. I should have been full of good cheer, too, but when they cut the cake some ugly part of me wanted Charles Heinz to go mental and be his old nasty self and threaten my mother with the rewedding cake knife in his hand until the police came and dragged him away. But nothing bad happened—in fact, at the end of the night I had to admit that the only bad things going on were the bad thoughts deep inside of me. The rewedding and the cheerfulness everyone felt was all about them, and I was like a grumpy little troll all hunched up in a corner thinking bad thoughts while dressed in a white tuxedo and sucking on a sour pickle.

4

TO DINE FOR

"Good morning, sleepyhead," Dad said as he gave my shoulder a shake. When I opened my eyes he handed me a can of Diet Coke. "Drink this. It will get your motor running."

"Mom doesn't let me drink that," I replied. "It makes me hyper. I can only have chocolate milk."

He leaned forward and made a sneaky-looking face. "What she doesn't know won't hurt her," he whispered, "so drink up. We have a huge day ahead of us."

Now that he was the big man of the house again I did what I was told and drank it down. It did get me going because a few minutes later I jumped out of bed, got dressed, and dashed into the kitchen.

"What's for breakfast?" I shouted. "I'm starving!"

Mom was sitting at the table with her chin propped up on her folded hands. She looked a little green and winced when I shouted. Her work friends had set up a private champagne bar in the ladies' powder room and she may have had too much fun at her own rewedding party. But not Dad. Since he had quit drinking he was full of energy this morning and in a great mood because this was the day he was going to unveil Mom's "unbelievable" rewedding gift.

"How about some scrambled eggs diner style?" he asked me, as he hovered over the stove top with a frying pan in his hand.

"You bet," I replied.

He began to crack the eggs into the pan and talk excitedly at the same time. "The gift I have for you is incredible," he said to Mom. "And it is big. Very BIG!" He waved the spatula over his head, flicking bits of half-cooked egg onto the floor.

Pablo and Pablita began to lap them up.

"Then how come you didn't give it to me on my rewedding day?" Mom asked. She sounded a bit annoyed.

Dad added some cheese and chopped-up ham and green peppers to the pan and worked them into the eggs. "Because," he joked, "I didn't want you *forgiving* me just for my money."

"Clever," Mom commented dryly. "You really have me figured out."

I didn't want them to get grumpy with each other after being remarried less than twenty-four hours, so I blurted out, "I really had a lot of fun at the rewedding."

"It was the best," Dad said warmly, and smiled at Mom as he set the eggs in front of me. She smiled back and blew him a kiss, but when she got a whiff of the eggs she pushed them away and stood up.

"I better get dressed," she said, and went up to their bedroom.

"Me, too," Dad added, and he followed her up the stairs.

I wolfed down the eggs and got myself ready, and in a few minutes we all left the house and walked down the front steps toward the car. The limo rental people had reclaimed the Hummer at dawn so we piled into what Dad called the "Heinzmobile," which was a President's Edition black Lincoln. The trunk was big enough to hold the Oval Office inside, and I thought that if I knocked on it Honest Abe himself would pop out and recite the Gettysburg Address.

"I like American cars, son," Dad announced. He turned the key and the engine backfired. The sound hurt my head. Maybe the car was haunted by John Wilkes Booth.

"When a car wears out," he continued, "you just throw it away and get another. Only in this country can we leave our past parked in a junkyard and drive off in a shiny new life. Tell me, where else in the world can you do that?"

"Do they have junkyards in Hawaii?" I asked.

He didn't hear me because he had ducked under the steering wheel to grab Pablo, who had gotten wedged under the brake pedal. When Dad came up he blindly handed him back to me. Pablo was upside down and wiggling his arms and legs like a crab. Pablita was sleeping on Mom's lap with her paws over her ears.

"Oh!" Dad suddenly cried out. "Guess who said this: 'Change is the law of life. And those who look only to the past or the present are certain to miss the future.' "

I had no idea.

He glanced at Mom. "Take a guess," he offered.

"God?" she said reluctantly, sounding tired.

"Nope. Freddy, your turn."

"The Hulk?"

"Nope. Here is a hint. He's one of our greatest presidents," he said, nearly chirping with happiness.

"Roosevelt?" Mom guessed, and then groaned as if talking was the same as being punched in the stomach.

"Nope."

"Washington?" I said. I really had no idea.

"Nope."

"Just tell us," Mom snapped. "I'm not feeling up to a pop quiz!"

"John F. Kennedy," Dad blurted out. "J.F.K.! He knew the power of *change*."

"And look where it got him," Mom replied under her breath, and gazed out her window at nothing in particular.

I thought maybe we were going to drive out to the new Diamond Warehouse store at the outlet mall and pick up a diamond the size of a fist to replace the tiny one Dad had given Mom before I was born. She told me she had pawned that one a long time ago and only received ten dollars for it because it was a "diamond chip."

"Like a tortilla chip?" I had asked, trying to imagine a ring that was also a snack.

"No," she replied, "it was like the size of a toenail clipping—probably one of his own." Back then she had laughed scornfully at the thought of him. I now wondered if she remembered telling me about the diamond chip or if bleaching her past had already erased all her old disappointments.

As we drove a few miles out of town we passed by chain restaurants, tourist motels, and farm stands, and when we stopped at a red light in front of Dutch Wonderland Family Amusement Park, Dad said offhand, "That would be a nice property to own."

"What do you mean?" I asked. In the distance a line of roller-coaster cars clacked up a hill of tracks, and when they plunged down the other side I could hear people scream. It made my head throb.

"Now that I'm a small business man," he said

smoothly as we continued down the highway, "I'd like to work my way up and own some blue-chip money-making properties." When he said that, Mom perked up and draped her arm over the seat where she made the big-money gesture by rubbing the tips of her thumb and pointer finger together. She winked slyly at me as if behind Dad's back she and I were in on something sneaky together, but that only made me nervous so I turned away and looked out the window at farmhands piling hay bales onto an old flatbed truck.

Just then we fishtailed off the highway and onto a rutted gravel parking lot which was skinned-looking where the black dirt showed through.

"Voilà!" Dad shouted after he hit the brakes and we skidded to a stop. "Isn't she a beauty?"

I was wrong about the rewedding gift being a diamond. It was an old silver roadside diner, and it looked like a dented-up can lying on its side with a wide ribbon wrapped around it and tied in a bow by the door.

Mom must have read my mind in more ways than one. "Why, it looks like a giant beer can waiting to be recycled," she remarked, and I noticed she now rubbed her ring finger with her thumb where she thought the big diamond would have fit.

Dad smiled broadly. "This old can is worth a lot more than a nickel," he said. "It's a gold mine!"

Mom made a mock angry face. "I'd rather just have the gold," she said.

He didn't take the hint. Instead, he sprang out of the car with the dogs chasing behind and began to run toward a hand-lettered sign on the front door that read:

OPENING SOON
UNDER NEW MANAGEMENT
MR. AND MRS. CHARLES HEINZ & SON

"Come on!" he hollered, waving madly at us to follow him. "Wait until you get a glimpse of your future."

We didn't have to wait long. As soon as he unlocked the front door the dogs dashed in and he directed us toward a mustard-colored booth he must have been using for an office because it was covered in neat piles of receipts and stacks of loser lottery tickets. Mom and I slid along the worn vinyl seat and Dad sat across the enamel tabletop from us. The sun shone in through a row of thick green-tinted windows. I glanced around at the half-dozen identical booths and the long greenish coffee counter with matching stools on polished chrome poles and the shiny griddle for cooking and the small open window where you could holler food orders in to the kitchen chef in back. Everything was neat and tidy and in its place just the way Dad liked it, and there was so much to see and do

I just felt like jumping up and taking orders and cooking and serving and cleaning and counting all that
money. I could feel it in my bones that I was born to
run a diner. I glanced at the dogs, and from the way
they were sitting next to the table watching Dad with
their bugged-out eyes I could tell they were as excited
as I was.

Dad rapped his knuckles on the table to get our attention. "It won't look like a beer can for long," he explained while squinting cleverly and tapping his finger
against his temple. "No, sir. After I won the money an
old friend helped put together a marketing plan so I
wouldn't blow my nest egg. Now, follow my thinking.
What is the busiest insect in the world?"

"Roach?" Mom guessed, glancing suspiciously toward the kitchen.

"Bee!" I blurted out.

"Right on!" Dad said, and gave me a high five. "So
we are going to call this place the Beehive Diner. Just
think of it painted in black and yellow stripes with a
bee face painted on one end and a pointy stinger on
the other. I can even have some black wings made out
of steel mesh and rivet them to the body."

I had to admit, this part of his plan sounded pretty
good.

Mom began to say something but Dad quickly held
up one finger to stop her. "Stay with me, Maria! Think
of the menu. We can have the Queen Bee Burger,

Peanut Butter and Royal Jelly, the Busy Bee on a Bun for the man on the run, a Beehive Breakfast Special served with Honeycomb cereal and Beebrain Coffee which will put a Bee in your Bonnet. The deal of the day could be the Bee-fore and After, where you get an appetizer, main course, and dessert. I mean, really, the *bee* possibilities are endless."

Mom tried again to say something and again Dad cut her off. "And if we get crowded, I'll just tell everyone to form a Bee-Line and wait to be seated. Oh, I couldn't beee more buzzed about this concept." He slapped the table so hard bits of paper flew into the air and the glass salt and pepper shakers hopped up and fell over. The dogs stopped licking at a greasy spot on the floor and ran off to hide under the counter.

Suddenly Mom bolted upright herself and looked pale enough to faint. "Where is the restroom?" she asked urgently.

"What's the matter?" I said.

"I'm afraid all this food talk has made me ill," she replied with a desperate look in her eyes as she scanned the room.

Dad pointed toward the far corner and I let her out of the booth. She walked as fast as a human could and didn't even get the narrow toilet door shut before we heard her throw up once, then again.

While we listened I felt real nervous and figured it was also because the beehive idea reminded me of when my brain got the best of me and my head felt like it was full of bees, and they were busy in ways that were bad for me.

"I don't have good experience with bees," I said to Dad.

"Then we'll see to it that this *is* a good experience and kick those past troubles behind," he said with complete confidence. "Yes, sir! You'll be a new man," he declared. "In no time at all you'll be wearing a name tag that reads *número uno* beekeeper."

I didn't quite know what to say, so I sat there in silence with a smile hanging on my face as if it, too, was a sign that read: UNDER NEW MANAGEMENT. All I knew was that my foot was tapping the floor as if I were pumping on the brakes to slow down my life so I could think about the hundred new things that were going on. Everything was happening so fast, plus it was time for me to get back on my meds.

In a moment we heard water running in the bathroom and finally Mom staggered out while drying her hands on a brown paper towel.

Dad hopped onto his feet and ran to help her. "Are you okay?" he asked quietly. He put one hand to her forehead but she brushed it away.

"I guess I just need some fresh air," she said, pulling herself together. "It's a little stuffy in here."

"That's perfect," he said. "Now I'll give you a tour of the house."

"What house?" Mom and I asked at the same time. I felt myself hop up before I even thought of hopping up. I was getting jumpy and I had that panic feeling in my belly like the diner was on fire and I couldn't find the exit.

"Can you believe this diner deal was so sweet a house came with it?" Dad announced, resting his hand on my shoulder. "The house is out back, so you can roll out of bed and roll into work. Not a moment is wasted. It is *bee-brilliant!*"

We followed him around the edge of the counter and through the galley kitchen and out a back door that had a window in it like a ship's porthole. Twenty feet away was a chunky little cottage that looked like it had once been a small barn. It had a black roof and red walls with black shutters on either side of the windows and bright green window boxes full of plastic yellow flowers. My first thought was that we should live in the diner and have the barn be the restaurant. I suggested it to Dad.

"No way," he replied. "Then the bee concept wouldn't work. You can't make the barn look like a bee." He gave me a look as if I were missing the point.

"I just mean," I tried to explain, "that there are all these farms around here, so a barn restaurant would fit right in. We could make it look Amish or something."

"Then people would think they'd have to sit down

with a bunch of bearded strangers and eat farm food like cows at a trough," he said, waving that thought away with his hand. "No, people want *fast food*. Bee-sting *fast*!" He jumped into the air and did a couple of twisty fast karate moves to demonstrate the power of his bee-sting speed.

Without thinking I skipped forward and gave him a straight karate kick in the knee.

"Ow!" he shouted, and frowned at me as he tilted forward and massaged his kneecap. "Why'd you do that?"

"Buzzzzz," I said, buzzing and wiggling my bee-sting bottom. I wasn't sure why I kicked him. Maybe I just needed to, or I really needed my meds. Either way, it wasn't good.

"Let's bee-have ourselves and go take a peek inside," Mom said impatiently as she gave me the evil eye. "I'm fading a little."

Dad fished the key out of his pocket and worked at unlocking the door, which he said was "tricky."

"Are you mad at me?" I whispered to Mom, and petted her hand.

"I'm just not myself this morning," she said quietly, and swallowed hard. "But I'll settle down. Don't worry."

"Me, too," I replied, and smiled as she squeezed my hand.

Finally Dad got the door unlocked. "Welcome to

honeycomb heaven," he announced with a bow, as if we were royalty. "Buzz on in."

"Buzzzzz," I said as Mom and I followed the dogs over the threshold. It was clean and tidy and after one second I loved it. There was a big living room with skylights over the old barn rafters and a hanging light fixture made out of welded-together horseshoes. Off the living room was a bedroom where Dad must have been staying before the rewedding because he still had a few of his things neatly folded up on the stripped mattress.

"Is there a room for me?" I asked, worried that I would have to sleep behind a shower curtain in the living room like Granny did at our house.

Dad smiled and pointed to a rough wood ladder propped up toward the back of the living room. "Your bedroom is the hayloft upstairs," he said. "Check it out, bee-boy."

I ran for the ladder and was halfway up when I turned around. "Mom, do you want to come up and see my new room with me?"

"Maybe later," she called back. "I'm just trying to find the most essential room in the house."

"Well, you won't find the kitchen," Dad said. "The diner is our kitchen."

"Don't say that word," Mom moaned. "I'm looking for the bathroom."

Dad must have pointed to a door in the bedroom and she trotted off and closed it behind her.

I kept climbing up to my room, which looked like it had once been an open hayloft but was now closed off with wide old boards up to the ceiling. At the top of the ladder I unlatched a door, stepped in, and closed it behind me. The room was empty and smelled of old pine trees and horse hay. It was a warm, friendly smell. On the far outside wall was a wide window that looked onto an oak tree that was bursting with fall colors. Beyond the tree was a field of harvested corn and past that stood a gleaming white Amish farm. The cornstalks were golden brown and large crows pecked at a few leftover ears. Milking cows grazed nearby in an open pasture. The sky was brilliant blue with just a few wispy clouds scribbling cursive nonsense overhead. I stared out at my new view of the world and felt better already, like a bee drunk on honey.

"Buzzzzz," I said again, and right away a thought popped into my mind. I wondered if I could open my heart and say to my dad, "I forgive you and I'm glad you're back," as Mom wanted me to. And if I said that, would my life on the inside start to look like that calm farm, all organized and purposeful and well run?

I stepped toward the window. A few leaves let go from the branches and slowly zigzagged down toward the ground. Right away it occurred to me that if I really did become Freddy Heinz, my Joey Pigza memories might all end up spread across the ground like the leaves, just waiting to be raked into a pile and burned. I figured then that Joey, too, would go up in smoke. I looked far into the sky and those wispy clouds seemed to spell out GOODBYE, JOEY as they drifted east. I could make it better for everyone, I thought, if I'd just step into their Heinz dream and go along with their plans. But something held me back.

Suddenly Dad clambered up the ladder. He flung my door open. "Hey, bee-boy," he said, a bit out of breath. "We have to get buzzing. Sorry to cut things short, but your mom got overexcited by her gifts and her tummy's way upset. She wants us to take her to the clinic." He grinned at me and I guessed he was grinning with pride because he thought his wedding present to Mom had made her sick with happiness.

"I'll be right down," I promised.

He left and I looked out at the sky for a few more seconds. I didn't want to leave, because in front of that window I didn't know if I was saying goodbye to Joey or hello to Freddy. But one way or the other, something in me was coming and going at the same time.

"Freddy!" Dad shouted. "¡Pronto!"

I jumped and at that moment I realized I was like an adopted kid who was getting used to a new name.

After we rounded up the dogs and got back into the

car I kept a sharp eye on Mom. She didn't say much, though she did give me a weak smile just to let me know she was okay.

But Dad was still excited. He talked about how he and Mom had first met years ago at a restaurant where he was the bartender and she was a waitress, so they knew the ropes. He said Mom could now leave the Beauty and the Beast Hair Salon for our own restaurant business where she could be a boss instead of a peon. He said he was learning some Spanish, too, and when he said a word of it he swaggered his shoulders proudly as if he had conquered one little part of that other language and now owned it.

When we got back to town we took Mom to the clinic and then stopped at the drugstore around the corner from our house on Plum Street. The pharmacist there knew us pretty well. Before Mom hopped out I whispered in her ear about getting my meds. "It's time," I said, not wanting Dad to hear me. "I feel like I'm buzzing all over on the inside."

She didn't make a sound but just nodded as if she already had it on her list, then she pushed the door open and went into the store by herself.

Once she was out of sight Dad turned around and smiled at me. "Wow," he said, wide-eyed. "Don't you just love it when life moves forward at the speed of light?"

"Not really," I said slowly. "I've lived like that before and it didn't work out so well because when you move too fast you don't always know where you'll end up."

"That's because I wasn't around to lead the way," he said. "But don't worry. This time I've got our future lined up in my sights."

He picked up Pablita and they stared at each other nose to nose.

"Let me guess," he pondered. "Your new name is Quesadilla. Am I right?"

Pablita whimpered and wiggled and Pablo clawed his way under the passenger seat.

5

OFF THE GRID

Ever since Mom had become Maria she thought she had become a good driver but she hadn't, and now she was behind the wheel of the Heinzmobile and speeding down the road. I had my helmet on and tightened my chin strap. Even though Mom and Dad had stopped making me wear my helmet around the house, I wanted extra protection in the car. We were on the way to my new school out past the diner and I was sitting next to her singing as loudly as possible a feel-good song I made up so I wouldn't think about how sad I was to leave my old school. "The gears in my head go round and round, round and round, round and round. The gears in my head go round and round, all the way to school. The holes in my head get big and wide, big and wide, big and wide. The holes in my head get big and wide, all the way to school. The rocks in my head—"

"Freddy!" she barked.

I ignored her.

"Freddy!" she barked again.

I ignored her again.

"Joey!"

I snapped to attention.

"Very funny," she said. "Did you take your meds?"

"This isn't about meds," I replied, rolling up my shirtsleeve so she could see the patch on my shoulder. "I'm just making up a song."

"Well, it's not a song I care for," she said. "I don't like it when you say bad things about yourself—especially on the way to a new school where I want you to make a good impression on the principal."

"The rocks in my head go crunch, crunch, crunch—"

"Freddy!"

I tilted my big helmeted head sideways and grinned. "Did you say something?" I asked calmly.

"Don't play these games with me," she said sternly. "If we're going to have a new life, we aren't going to repeat those old ways."

"Well, I don't want to go to a new school," I said, getting to the point because that is what was really bothering me. "I liked my old school and it liked me."

"We've already talked about this. Now that we are

moving to the diner, you have to change schools," she replied. "But you'll adjust in no time."

"But I'm doing well at the school I'm in," I stressed, and I felt a lump building in my throat. "I like Mr. Turner, and after I've worked so hard to pull myself together I just want everything to stay the same." I covered my face with my hands because the tears came before I could turn away. "I'm Joey Pigza," I said, "and I want to stay Joey Pigza. I don't want to be Freddy Heinz. I don't even know who he is. Who knows? He could be worse than my bad old self."

Mom reached over and put her hand around my shoulder. "Honey, Freddy Heinz can be whoever you want him to be. For instance, let me tell you about Freddy's mom, Maria Heinz. She is way different from Fran Pigza. She's a confident woman and a positive thinker. She's in love and in a happy marriage. She no longer allows her Pigza limitations to overshadow her new talents. She is reaching for the stars. *See*," she said proudly, "aren't you impressed with how much I've grown?"

I wiped my eyes on my sleeves. "I don't want to rock the boat," I sniffed. "I just want to be me."

"Just because you change your name doesn't mean you have to completely change who you are on the inside," she said.

"I don't think that's true," I replied. "I think if I forgive Dad I'll no longer be Joey, because Joey wouldn't forgive him. Only Freddy would, and once he does then life as I know it is over for me."

"And isn't that the entire point?" Mom proclaimed as she reached across and poked me on the shoulder. "That life as you *knew* it will be over and life as you *know* it will begin?"

"Can I get into an ugly name-calling argument with you about this?" I asked.

"No," she insisted. "I'm your parent and I'm telling you what is best for you, and at this moment it is best that you are Freddy Heinz in the process of transferring to a new school. Got that?"

"I don't understand why you are being nice to Dad and doing whatever he wants and you are mean to me," I said.

"That's easy. I'm nice to whoever is nice to me," she replied. "And I'm mean to whoever is mean to me. It's as simple as that!" She snapped her fingers, then suddenly yelped and swung the steering wheel to the right. As we squealed toward the school driveway she hit the curb. I jerked sideways and banged my head on the window.

"Good thing I was wearing my helmet," I said, rapping on it with my knuckles.

"Yeah," she cracked, throwing the car into reverse and pulling away from the curb. "Or you'd be singing, The lumps on my head go ouch, ouch, ouch!"

She shifted into drive, hit the gas, and the Heinzmobile heaved itself forward and into a space for disabled drivers.

"You can't park here," I insisted, and pointed to the blue-and-white sign.

"Yes I can," she replied, and pointed to my helmet.

"I'm not disabled!" I protested.

"You will be if you don't straighten up and act like a normal kid," she said, and made a fist.

She unsnapped the helmet and lifted it off, then reached over and tousled my matted hair. "Maybe I should dye your hair red," she speculated. "Then we'd match."

"Please don't make me look like a flaming marshmallow," I begged, and put the helmet back on. "I don't want the principal to see the dent in my head."

"Suit yourself," Mom replied. "Personally, I think the dent is cute."

We walked up the sidewalk and entered the front door. The school was a lot newer than my beat-up old one in town, and Mom pointed out every fancy detail—the easy-to-open doors, the freshly waxed floors, the big picture windows, the brightly painted walls, and the colorful bulletin boards covered with a display of cut-out Thanksgiving turkeys and pumpkins and Pilgrims' hats and shoes. "Even the air smells nice and minty," she remarked, taking a deep breath.

"If you like it so much why don't you work here?" I asked. "You could teach a class in toenail sculpting."

"Don't get testy with me," she said under her breath. "This is not the time to debate who is the parent and who is the child. Got that?"

I got it.

We entered the front office and Mom introduced herself as she signed the visitors' log.

"The principal is expecting you, Mrs. Heinz," the secretary replied as she stood up. "She's just finishing up her morning rounds. You can wait in her office."

I looked at Mom's signature: *Mrs. Maria Heinz.* Even her handwriting had changed. Her letters used to look crammed together like a row of bad teeth, but now they were neat and evenly spaced. Then as clearly as I could I wrote down "Joey Pigza, a.k.a. Freddy Heinz" in huge loopy letters while Mom followed the secretary down a hallway. I caught up just when the secretary pushed open a door and stepped aside, allowing us to enter first. "Take a seat," she offered, and gestured toward two swivel chairs, before disappearing up the hall.

Mom posed herself with a smile so bright it looked as if her entire face had just been buffed with wood polish. She was so shiny I spun away and looked at the wall. There was a row of glossy photographs of plump little babies dressed up like bees in black-and-gold Pittsburgh Steelers outfits. They were doing cute things. One bee baby was sitting in a giant helmet with a jar of honey. Two of them were having a tug-of-war over a football. The last photo had a baby bee clutching his black-and-gold diaper with a desperate look on his face. Below it a caption read, "I hope I make it to the goal line!"

Dad was right about the bee theme, I thought. It's everywhere.

"Haven't we waited long enough?" I asked a minute after we sat down. "We can come back tomorrow."

"Settle down," Mom said, and her glowing, posed expression sagged. "We just got here."

There was a Pittsburgh Steelers paperweight on the principal's desk and I reached out for it. The moment I touched it Mom slapped my hand. "Hands to yourself," she hissed. "You know better."

"Joey does, but Freddy doesn't," I sang, reaching for it again.

"Don't mess with me," she said brusquely. "Now get with the program."

Suddenly we both heard footsteps marching down the hallway.

"Here she comes," Mom whispered as she regained her pose. "Let me do the talking, and if you behave yourself I'll tell you a secret." She arched her eyebrow which meant it was a good one. But I couldn't ask her more about it, because at that moment the principal breezed in and smiled warmly at both of us.

"I'm Mrs. Ginger," she said.

"Maria Heinz," Mom replied. "A pleasure to meet you."

"And you must be our new student," Mrs. Ginger said, smiling broadly as she reached toward my hand, which I had already stuck out. She seemed very nice except that when our fingers touched she gave me a static electric shock.

"Yipes," I yelped, and examined my palm as if I had been stung by a bee.

Mom tugged on my shoulder and whispered, "You can sit down now." Then in an extra small whisper she said, "Stay focused."

I plopped down and noticed that Mrs. Ginger's lips were pressed together as she began to examine me in a very thoughtful way.

"I'm puzzled," she said, and rapidly typed some information into the computer on her desk. "Over the phone you said you moved here from Philadelphia, but their system doesn't show any school records for a Freddy Heinz. Are you sure you gave me the correct information?"

"Let me think," Mom said, and she reached for my hand and squeezed it, which was our signal for me to keep my mouth shut. "Of course," she chirped as if suddenly remembering an important detail. "He was homeschooled some of last year and that must have thrown the paperwork off."

"Not likely," Mrs. Ginger replied. "The paperwork on a student stays in the system for many years before it gets archived."

There was an awkward silence as Mrs. Ginger stared directly at Mom while Mom stared back. Neither one of them spoke, but after a while Mrs. Ginger's magnetic gaze was too strong for Mom and it began to pull the words right out of her mouth.

"Well," Mom said hesitantly, "we really didn't get any paperwork on the homeschooling, which didn't work out too well, so I think it might be better if Freddy repeats a grade."

"Without records we'll have to test him to find what level he falls into," she explained.

"But I'm at least sixth grade!" I blurted out.

"How old are you?" she asked.

"I'm small for my age," I said, then turned to Mom. "How old is Freddy?"

"You know your age," she said, and glowered.

"Well," Mrs. Ginger said before Mom and I could get into an argument in front of her. "It doesn't really matter what age you are. What matters are your skill levels, and the test will determine that."

"Do me a favor," I said to her. "Check for a kid named Joey Pigza in Lancaster." I reached toward her computer to turn the screen so I could see the list of student names and point mine out to her.

Mrs. Ginger softly clamped down on my hand. "I'm

sorry," she said, and switched her computer to a blank screen. "We are not allowed to share the confidential records of other people."

"But I am that other person," I argued a little too loudly.

She then looked at Mom as if expecting an explanation, but Mom only gave her a "Beats me" shrug as she put her hand on my shoulder.

"Freddy," Mom said calmly, "we can talk about this later."

Then she turned her poised gaze toward the principal. "Freddy can begin tomorrow if you are ready for him."

"That will be fine," Mrs. Ginger replied. "I'll have the curriculum coordinator arrange the tests." She passed Mom a folder. "Just fill out these enrollment forms and return them with Freddy."

Just then the secretary knocked on the door and without waiting stuck her head into the office. "I'm sorry," she said to Mom, then turned to the principal. "Mrs. Ginger, we need you out here for a minute."

In the background I could hear a kid arguing and he was saying just what I was thinking.

"You can't do this to me! NO! No! No!"

"Just for fifteen minutes," someone said. Maybe it was his teacher.

Mrs. Ginger stood up quickly. "Excuse me for a moment," she said firmly. "There is always a fire to put out with this job."

The moment she left Mom uncrossed her legs and hopped up. "I've got to run to the ladies' room for a moment," she whispered.

"You made me look weird," I said.

"You did that to yourself," she replied, and tapped me on the helmet. "You can't go around being Freddy for one moment, and then being Joey the next."

"Well, I'm not Freddy," I said.

"You are, and you better get used to it," she said. "Now behave yourself." She took her purse and was out the door in two steps.

I gave her a head start, then slipped out the door and walked toward where I heard the kid yelling. I wanted to see what they did to a bad kid at Keystone Elementary because already I felt out of place. I stood by the door and pressed my ear to it. I heard a lot of people talking at once. Then the door opened a bit and I saw a kid sitting in a big chair and he was kicking his legs back and forth and his face kept switching from sad to angry then sad to angry. It was like someone was flicking a light switch on and off real fast, then suddenly a hand gripped me on the shoulder.

"Excuse me," Mrs. Ginger said sharply. "Is there something I can help you with?"

"Ah, yes," I shot back. I didn't really have a question

to ask so I just said the first thing that came to my mind. "There is something you can help me with. Are people angry because they don't get what they want? Or don't get who they are?"

"What do you mean?" she asked.

"I mean, I'm upset because I used to be one kid then overnight became another, so I can no longer be the kid I used to be and yet I don't know who I am."

"That is very interesting," she replied. "Can you tell me about this other person you think you are?" She looked at me in the same magnetic way she had looked at Mom, and I could feel my brain was wearing itself out with trying to figure how I could prove who I was. But I was just a regular kid and I didn't have a wallet or a license or a Social Security card or a passport or a birth certificate. All I had was the truth, but that wasn't good enough.

When I didn't say anything her expression relaxed and she looked at me with that kind, sympathetic look, which right away told me she thought I was slow or confused in some invisible way. In that split second I understood that if she knew I had been in special ed she would always think there was something wrong with me. Even after I had changed, other people's opinions of me wouldn't change.

"How did you get that helmet?" she asked, touching it with the tip of her finger.

"When I was Joey Pigza I dove out the top floor window," I replied. "But Freddy is okay now. The dent is getting better."

She leaned forward and asked very softly, "Where is your mother?"

Just then Mom spotted us and dashed up the hall with a nervous look on her face.

"Freddy was just telling me a little more about being someone else named Joey Pigza," Mrs. Ginger said as she reached for Mom's hand.

"Oh," Mom said, smiling awkwardly. "That's just his imaginary friend."

"I see," Mrs. Ginger said. "We have a wide range of programs here, Mrs. Heinz, so I don't want you to worry about Freddy's special *needs*." Then she turned to me and patted my shoulder and I caught her eyes pulling toward the clock over a drinking fountain.

"Come on, Freddy," Mom said in a voice that did not want to be questioned. "We've got some change-of-school shopping to do."

Neither of us said a word until we climbed into the car, but we must have been thinking in our silence. As soon as she closed her door she said, "Don't you get it? A new name at a new school will mean no one will know about your special-ed past. Won't that be a relief?"

"I guess," I said. "Though my past doesn't bother me as much as it seems to bother other people. And from the way you treated me just now I bet this principal thinks I'm a nut."

"Well, you can't go around telling her that you are two different people. That usually attracts the wrong kind of attention," she advised. "You should just stick with the program and be Freddy Heinz."

"Okay, okay," I said. "I'll try. Now, what is the secret?"

She smiled and I could tell she was just as happy as I was to find a new topic. "Well, here's a surprise that can't be changed," Mom said. "It's pretty amazing."

"Well?" I asked. "I'm waiting."

She reached for my hand and held it palm down against her belly and rubbed it back and forth.

"If you are going to be sick again, please open the window," I said in a bit of a panic.

"You don't understand," she said calmly, looking intently into my eyes. "There is going to be another little Heinz in the family."

"Huh?" I said. I was a little confused because I was waiting for her to throw up in my direction.

"A baby," she said, smiling widely. "I'm pregnant."

"You mean another Pigza?"

"No," she said, "this one is a Heinz."

"You mean I'm going to have a brother?" I asked. "Or a sister?"

"In about five or six months," she said. "Your dad and I have been seeing each other for a while, you know, and I guess—"

"Do you know what it will be?" I interrupted, not wanting to hear the details.

"Not yet," she replied. "I don't want to know till I see it."

"That'll be a surprise," I said, wide-eyed.

"The best kind of surprise," she agreed.

I smiled and the happiness was like turning your face toward the glowing sun on the first day of spring. The warmth spread all the way through me from my nose to my toes.

"I'll be a brother," I whispered. "I love that idea."

"Oh, one more thing," she said, holding up a finger. "Let's keep this secret between ourselves. Charles is really eager to tell you first."

"It'll be our secret," I said, and reached over and again put my hand flat against her belly.

"I bet it's a boy," I predicted. "I bet it's the *perfecto* boy you always wanted."

"I already have the perfect boy I've always wanted," she said, smiling and scratching the top of my helmet as if it were my head. "If it's a boy, I'll just be getting a second helping of what I love best."

She started the car.

"Be careful," I warned her, and tapped on her belly as she put the car in reverse. "That's a lot more than an imaginary friend in there."

6

IN THE BAG

The next morning I got up early and dressed in the nice new school clothes Mom and I had picked out while shopping. I wanted to make a better "Freddy" impression at school. But at home I could still be me, so I put on a Halloween "Bloody Head" Chef hat I had found on a clearance table because Halloween was long gone. It was really a great-looking hat because there was a bloody plastic meat cleaver stuck in it. When I showed it to Mom, she smiled and said, "It reminds me of you."

As soon as I put it on the next morning I wanted to chop up food and start cooking. I hustled over to the diner and began to make pancakes, eggs, and sausages. I needed lots of energy for school, plus it was up to me to make sure Mom was eating well because now I knew she was eating for two. I arranged

the food on a tray along with her orange juice and vita-
mins. I decorated it with a plastic red rose in a little
vase and carried it to the house.

"Room service from the brain-dead chef," I called
out as I knocked on her bedroom door. "One special
bee-sting breakfast for one special queen bee!"

"Please leave it on the floor, honey, and I'll get it in
a second," she replied. "I just stepped out of the
shower."

"Yes, ma'am," I snappily replied, and I set the tray
down. The dogs smelled the food and came running,
but before they could even touch the tray with their little pink tongues I tackled them. "No dog germs for my
brother or sister," I whispered into their twitching
ears. "I don't want the kid coming out behaving like
you two gremlins."

I carried them back into the diner and set them
down on a little bed I had made out of old flour sacks
I had found in the pantry.

Dad was up and still wearing his blue-and-white-
striped silk pajamas, but he was not goofing off. He already had a wet tootbrush and a box of baking soda
and was going from booth to booth as he cleaned all
the clogged holes in the tops of the salt and pepper
shakers.

"Can I help?" I asked. "You can teach me how to be
a clean freak."

He glanced up at me and shook his head back and

forth when he saw my costume. "Not now," he grunted as he worked on a stubborn speck of dirt. "Cleaning relaxes me so my mind can think of other things, like more winning lottery numbers."

I knew what he meant because whenever I gave the dogs a bath I was always thinking of other things—like *not* giving the dogs a bath.

As I stood there he suddenly dropped the tooth-brush and pulled a pencil from behind his ear and scratched some numbers down on a piece of paper. He must have liked what he wrote because he whistled after he read them out loud. "Hello, you beautiful money magnets!" he sang. Then he put the pencil back behind his ear, slipped the paper into his pajama pocket, and went back to scrubbing.

I watched him do this a bunch of times in a row while I hovered over the grill flipping the lard-clotted Brillo pad I had used to scrub down the griddle. As I practiced double and triple flips I perfected my new grill-master signature saying.

"Do you want fries with that?" I yelled at my blurry reflection in the chrome panel over the grill.

"Are you talking to me?" I asked myself in a deep voice.

"I said," waving the spatula over my bloody hat, "Do you want *fries* with that?"

"What'd you say?" Dad asked.

"Do you want fries with that?" I hollered back.

"Could you pipe down? I'm trying to tune in some lucky lottery numbers," he said, sounding exasperated. "If we're ever to own a major theme park, I've got to hit the mega lottery big-time."

"Sorry," I replied, then stooped down and whispered to Pablita, "Do you want fries with that?"

Just then I heard a loud yelp followed by Pablo running from around the corner with a mouse glue trap stuck on his nose. He must have poked his pointy snout right on it. While I tried to remove it without peeling his nose off, Pablita stared at him like what he did was really stupid. If she were suddenly human I expect she would stand up on her hind legs, prop her front paws on her hips just like Mom does, and say, "You only have yourself to blame!"

Just when I got the trap off his nose Mom arrived with her tray. "From now on I could have pancakes every morning," she said as she lifted my gruesome hat and kissed me on the head. "But let's hold off on the sausage and eggs, okay?"

"Room service is open twenty-four hours a day," I said, beaming. "You can count on me."

"I won't forget that," she replied, then picked up the coffee pot and two cups. I followed her to where Dad was slowly writing out a list of numbers. She poured a cup for him and one for herself.

"A little caffeine will light up those winning numbers in your head," she said, briskly massaging his scalp with her freshly sculpted fingernails. They looked like ten black-and-yellow bees.

"Maybe if you just beat the side of your head really hard on the edge of the table," I suggested, "a winning number will drop out of your ear."

"Or maybe if you start juggling real meat cleavers you'll look like that for the rest of your life," Dad snapped back as he glared at me.

"Sorry," I replied in a small voice. "I think this hat has left me with half a brain."

"No, I'm the one who should be sorry," he said, and took a deep breath. "I'm just tense from *thinking* so hard." He blew on his hot coffee before he took a little sip. "It was after I changed my name and got my new outlook on life that I got some karma points and won the lottery. But lately I've been on a losing streak, and now I'm thinking all that karma was used up and I have to get some fresh karma."

Mom rolled her eyes.

"How?" I asked, trying to be more helpful.

"Like give away free turkey dinners to people who don't have food of their own," he continued.

"That sounds like a lot of work," Mom commented. "Besides, can we really afford to give our money away?"

"It won't cost much," he reasoned. "And with all the good karma, we could make a fortune."

"Should we hire staff?" Mom suggested. "That's a big job."

"Freddy will help me," Dad said, and smiled at me. "Won't you, son?"

"You mean Joey?" I said right back in his face.

"You know very well that Freddy is the new Joey," he replied. "So stop acting so stubborn."

"But what about school?" I asked, looking toward Mom. "We were supposed to go back today."

She glanced at Dad and I followed her eyes, which were full of concern.

"Well," he said, and scratched his head. "Last night your mom was telling me she got a pretty bad vibe from Mrs. Ginger, so we began to consider some new, fresh thoughts about your education. We started thinking big, like we do in the Heinz family. You see, here is how the world runs for the truly smart, rich people. For them school is only for kids without jobs. But if you have a job already, then you can just skip right over school like I pretty much did and graduate to having a real life. You learn more by doing than by sitting on your rear all day long learning things you'll never use. I didn't go to school much and look at me." He tapped himself on the chest. "I turned out pretty good and I've got nothing but unlimited potential as Charles Heinz. And not only will you make money, you'll learn how to go from being a boy to being a man."

I liked the part about making money and about becoming a man, but even I knew what he was saying about not going to school was crazy because it sounded like something I would cook up.

"Are you sure?" I asked suspiciously. "All kids go to school."

"No way," he shot back. "Farm kids get off to help their families with the harvest, so why not you, too? I need you here to help *harvest* some money in the diner."

"Mom, are you sure about this?" I asked.

She stared into her coffee and took a sip. "Let's try it for a few months until we get the diner up and running. After the holidays we'll look for a private school where you can start the second half of the year. But for now your dad needs your help around here."

"But you always said school was important," I reminded her.

"Not more important than family," she said decisively. "Now, you can either stay home and help your family or take a chance on your tests with Mrs. Ginger and possibly repeat sixth grade, maybe fifth grade. Who knows, they may even have you repeat *fourth* grade."

"No way I'm doing that," I declared. "I'll stay here with you guys and work."

"That's the smart choice," Dad said with enthusiasm. "The Heinz choice." He gave me a big wink and a thumbs-up.

"Well, how can I help?" I asked. "I'm ready to do some *real* homework."

"First things first," Dad stated. "Here's the plan. We need to clear out the Plum Street house for some renters. It won't take us long to get rid of all our old personal stuff, and then we'll dash back here and get busy with the Busy Bee."

"And I need to go shopping," said Mom, "so you can drop me at the mall on the way."

"Are you sure you don't want to stay home and *rest*?" Dad asked, and patted his stomach.

I knew what he was trying to say but I kept my mouth shut because knowing about little Heinzie was a secret I had with Mom.

"No," she replied. "I feel fine and we need to pick up some new things for this house since we're leaving the other place furnished."

"That's what I call teamwork," Dad said, and clapped his hands together. "We'll make the money and you can spend it."

"Don't be a smart you-know-what," Mom said playfully. "All the good karma you earn from treating me like an earth angel will lead you to a million bucks."

Dad didn't say another word as he strolled off to put on some work clothes. I dashed up to my loft bedroom, where I quickly changed into my jeans. I took off the bloody chef hat and felt more like myself again. I climbed back down my ladder and rounded up the dogs. I gave them each a biscuit then slammed the front door and ran to the Heinzmobile. In a few bee-sting fast minutes we had dropped Mom off at the mall and returned to the Plum Street house.

After I walked up the steps I hesitated at our old front door. Dad put his hand on my shoulder.

"Let me give you a bit of fatherly advice," he said, and pushed the door open. "This will be a lot easier if you think of yourself as Freddy."

"It would really be easy if I didn't have to do it at all," I replied.

"But you do," he insisted, and pressed a box of black garbage bags into my hands. "And if you pretend you are Freddy then it will be a piece of cake getting rid of all your stuff because Joey will just be some stranger to you."

At that moment I had a peculiar feeling, like I was an undertaker going into a house where someone was dead and I had to go pull out the body and put it into a bag. But I didn't say anything to Dad. I took a deep breath and held it as I lowered my chin and stepped into the house and marched directly into my bedroom.

It took me a while to get warmed up to throwing all my stuff away. At first I had to hold each thing in my hand and remember where I got it and what it meant to me and anything I had ever done with it. Only then could I toss it in the bag. I did that with a few things until I was tired from remembering every teensy detail of every button, shoelace, marble, or whatever it was that I touched. Finally I began to pick up the pace and then once I got going there was no stopping me. I tossed away the books that had my name in them and all my photographs. I ripped the posters and pictures off my wall and balled them up and shoved them in the bag. I even threw away the "Get Well, Joey" cards my class from school had sent me. Maybe they'll think I died from my head injury, I thought, since I'll never see them again. I threw away my bedsheets and pillows. I gathered up my stuffed animals and tossed them into a bag. I went into my closet and threw away all my games and toys from the top shelf. I shoved in all the clothes, except for one shirt, which stopped me in my tracks. It was my baseball jersey that Dad had given me which had PIGZA spelled across the back. It was my favorite shirt and it was faded and soft and it smelled like cut grass and dirt and sweat.

I pulled the jersey on over my T-shirt and went into the kitchen where Dad was emptying some cupboards.

"Can I keep this?" I asked in a small voice. I had my back to him so he could see the PIGZA name across my shoulders.

"In the bag!" he ordered. "Just like the rest of this cruddy old junk." I turned toward him and he pointed to a mountain of lumpy bags piled up in the living room. "You have to get rid of the old to make way for the new—everyone knows that."

"It's hard to get rid of stuff you love," I said. "Especially when it has your name on it. I promise I'll never wear it out in public. I'll hide it under my mattress."

"Trust me," he insisted. "The more you throw away, the easier it gets. I threw away all my old Pigza stuff—shoes, undies, socks—the whole shebang, and I never felt better."

"But don't you remember when we played baseball together?" I pleaded.

"Nope," he replied.

"You were the coach!" I reminded him. "You even got a tattoo of my jersey on your arm!"

"That was the old Carter Pigza," he said as he pulled up his T-shirt sleeve.

The tattoo was gone and replaced with a fleshy scar. I stood there with my mouth hanging open.

He smiled like a smug cat. "I'm Charles Heinz now. And you are Freddy. Got that? Now let's move on."

"You can't possibly believe you are Charles Heinz," I said, sputtering a bit. "I mean, that's crazy."

"But I am Charles," he replied, and shifted his eyes toward a wall mirror to look at himself.

"Look me in the eye when you say that," I said. "Eye to eye."

"Man to man," he said. "I'm Charles and you are

Freddy, and just as you are erasing all traces of Joey I erased Carter."

"Well, I know I'm not really Freddy," I said. "So you can't really be Charles."

"It *really* hurts me to hear you say that," he said softly. "All you have to do is stop being so stubborn about being Joey and join the Heinz family. You might as well get it over with because things are moving ahead faster than you think."

"Then I'll wait until later," I said glumly.

"Good enough," he replied, satisfied that I was getting a little closer to seeing things his way. "Now, give me the shirt."

He stuck out his hand. I pulled the shirt off over my head, balled it up, and tossed it to him. Then before I could see him stuff it in a bag I turned around and stomped back to my room.

I was pouting when he came in but he ignored my mood because he wanted that to change, too.

"Wow," he said, surveying the empty room. "You should be happy now that you have been liberated from your junky old past."

"I guess," I said.

"Can you keep a secret?" he asked, looking at himself in the cracked mirror over the dresser.

"Yeah," I replied, even though keeping a secret was really hard for me to do. Maybe that's why I wasn't so good at faking being somebody else.

"Not a word to your mom," he whispered, "but one of these days I'm going to take things a step further and surprise her by having this old face worked on."

"Really?" I asked. "Like a nose job?"

"More than that," he said, gently patting his cheeks. "A complete do-over. Someday I won't just be acting like a whole new man, I'll remove the bandages from my face and I'll look like one, too."

"Is this how big-time criminals change their identities?" I asked.

"Nah, it's how big-time winners upgrade their looks," he replied. He reached into his back pocket and pulled out his wallet. He flipped it open and removed a picture of a movie star he had ripped out of a magazine. "See this guy's face?" he said, tapping on the paper. "There is nothing money can't buy."

"What about me?" I asked.

"When you turn sixteen," he said. "Anything you want. You can have a new car and a dimple put into the middle of your chin. If you want to look like Elvis—"

"Can I get little horns on my forehead?" I blurted out. "I saw a picture of a guy who had horn implants and he looked cool."

"Negative!" he said firmly. "No Heinz is going to have horns on my watch. You might run for president someday and you can act like you have horns but you can't actually have them. There are limits, you know. Now let's get going."

We dragged the trash bags from my room out to the trunk of the Heinzmobile. We took them up the road and beyond the railroad bridge to a Goodwill collection box then returned for the next room. It took us four loads, and when we were finished Dad taped a note on the front door with the key in it for the new renters.

As I walked down the steps I muttered to myself, "*Adiós, Casa Pigza.*"

I could just imagine the house replying, "*Buena suerte*, Joey."

In the car, Dad was sweating. "That was more work than I thought it would be," he sighed, and popped open the last Diet Coke from the refrigerator. "Man, I need a breather."

7

FAST FOO

I was standing at the edge of the diner parking lot holding my coat in my hands as I watched Mom's taxi drive down the road toward Lancaster. When I had first heard the taxi pull up across the gravel and beep its horn I grabbed my coat and helmet from the house and ran to the driveway because I wanted to ride along with her and talk about little Heinzie. It was still our secret from Dad that I knew about the baby, so Mom and I couldn't talk about it with him buzzing around us all the time. But when I reached the parking lot Mom was already in the taxi. I tapped on the window and after she rolled it down she told me to stay and help Dad.

"But I want to be with you so we can *talk*," I said.

"We'll talk later," she whispered as if he were around the corner. "But right now he needs your help.

Besides, I'm just going to be shopping for baby clothes all day after I see the doctor."

"I love to shop for baby clothes," I said.

"No you don't," she replied. "You have the patience of a gnat when it comes to shopping."

She was right. "Okay," I said glumly. "I'll see you later."

"Go in the house and ask your dad what you can do to make some money," she said, and winked at me. "He's loaded."

Now that I wasn't going to school anymore it made sense that I should spend my time making money. I went into the diner and ditched my coat and helmet. Dad was standing in front of the coffee counter with one hand on his hip and the other gripping a soda.

"For ten bucks I'll get down on my hands and knees and scrub the diner floor," I suggested.

"I already did it," he replied, pointing down at the gleaming linoleum. "When I can't sleep at night I like to scrub."

"I'll reorganize the food pantry for five bucks," I offered.

"Did it two nights ago," he said. "You will now find that all the supplies are in alphabetical order. I've also inventoried the glassware, dishes, cutlery, and cooking pots, so I know what we'll need before we open."

"I'll clean out the grease traps then," I shot back. "I'm not afraid to get dirty."

"Been there, done that," he replied.

"Then what can I do to make some cash?" I asked, feeling frustrated. "You know, to work at the diner like you said?"

He was ready for that question.

"I was just standing here thinking. Every person has a special talent in life," he said slowly as he pulled a roll of bills from his pocket. He peeled a ten from the pack and laid it real nice and easy onto the palm of my outstretched hand.

"That's more like it," I said, smiling brightly. "So what is my special talent?"

"I couldn't sleep the other night," he said, "and then I was stung with a brilliant idea!"

Before I knew it I was dressed in a fuzzy black-and-yellow bee costume and standing out in front of the diner on the side of Highway 30. The head on the bee costume was so huge that Dad had to tape it to the bee body to keep it from falling off. I had a huge cardboard sign nailed to a stick, which I waved back and forth as cars passed.

COMING SOON!
BEEHIVE DINER FAST FOO

Dad had run out of room on the sign, so there was no D on *food*. When I pointed that out to him he just tapped the side of his head and said slyly, "When people see the mistake it will make them look *twice*. One of the great rules of advertising is that there is no such thing as bad publicity." Below *FOO* he had written in smaller letters, NO JOB? NO MONEY? EAT THANKSGIVING DINNER FOR FREE—NOON TO THREE! It seemed to me that a car would have to be creeping along at about two miles an hour to read our free invitation.

"You drum up business," he had said, putting the sign in my hand. "I've got some new numbers to play. Then I'll make a food supply run and pick up your mom downtown." He got into the Heinzmobile. "And remember, hardworking little honeybees harvest good karma for the hive. See you later, bee-boy!" he yelled as his tires kicked up gravel. "Good luck!"

Trying to sell BEEHIVE DINER FAST FOO might have broken that rule about no such thing as bad publicity. I waved the sign over my head and desperately tried to get drivers to notice me, but they seemed to either steer away from me and nearly hit oncoming cars or aim for me. The more I jumped around and waved my sign the hotter it got inside the costume, and before long sweat was rolling down my skin. Finally, with each passing car, I seemed to lose a little bit of my mind. After a few hours I was running into the middle of the road and swinging my sign and shouting at cars, "I'm a killer bee! Don't mess with meeee!" Then I'd go running back to the side and hop up and down as if I were an escapee from a Beehive Mental Asylum.

It was time to take a lunch break. I buzzed off, and about five bee-sting-fast minutes later I was standing in our parking lot, shoving a box of Oreos I found in the "O" section of the diner pantry into my mouth. Suddenly a lady driver pulled in and slowed as she came toward me. I stepped aside as the car inched to a stop. The driver leaned toward me and I pressed my giant bee head against the outer edge of the window. "Buzz-buzz," I said, and bits of cookie sprayed from my mouth.

"Are you guys finally going to open?" she asked.

To my surprise it was Mrs. Ginger. She was wearing a sweater with a bee appliqué on it.

"Yeah," I said nervously, just waiting for her to say something to me about not returning to school even though it was a Saturday. But with my costume on she didn't recognize me.

"Great," she said. "I've been waiting, 'cause I love bees."

"We are serving up a free Thanksgiving dinner next week," I said. "So if you know anyone who wants some, send them on over."

"That's thoughtful," she said. "I'm sure I can steer a few people in your direction."

"Gotta go," I said, and began to back away. In a moment she waved and drove on and I went back to work.

It was more of the same. When there were no cars I

leaned on my sign and caught my breath, but as soon as a car was in sight I'd lurch back into the road again. Just as cars wanted to splat me against their windshields like a big fat bug, I wanted to swat them with my sign. Drivers looked scared then angry as they steered around me. I got so steamed up I bent over and waved my stinger at them. And the more irritated they looked the more I felt like a killer bee.

Just then a guy in a little car that looked like a circus car squeezed his ah-*uga* horn and scared me half to death. Without thinking, I picked up a rock and threw it at him with so much force it struck his clown car on the rear bumper. Instantly the guy hit the brakes.

"That not *bee* good," I buzzed out loud to myself when I saw his reverse lights come on. I dropped the sign then turned and made a beeline into the diner, locked the door, and dove under a booth.

A minute later the angry guy hammered on the glass door with my sign. In a muffled voice I heard him yell, "Come on out, you little costumed criminal."

I didn't, and after a few minutes of threatening to rip my wings off he tossed the sign aside and left.

I crawled out from under the table. "I need another break," I said out loud, and rubbed dirt off my fur. I still had my ten bucks so I thought I would walk down to Dutch Wonderland theme park and chill out. I had done enough work for one day. But when I tried to take the costume off I couldn't reach the zipper in the back. What the heck, I thought, I'll fit right in at a theme park and do some advertising on the way.

I went outside and picked up the sign and carried it for the fifteen minutes it took to walk to the entrance of Dutch Wonderland. Even though the outside air was cool, the temperature was about a million degrees inside my costume. I couldn't ask anyone to pull the zipper down and help me out of the costume because I only had on my undershorts. All I could think about doing was going down the Log Flume ride and getting soaked. But when I reached the ticket window it was twenty-three bucks to get into the park. "How about half a day?" I asked.

"Nope, it's a whole day or nothing," said the girl, who was dressed like a Dutch milkmaid.

"Give me a break," I said, looking at a notice taped to the window. "It's the last weekend before you close for winter."

"Rules are rules," she said pertly.

"I'll give you some honey," I offered.

"Buzz off," she snapped, "or I'll call an exterminator."

I spun around and went back to the parking lot. The front of the park was shaped like a castle, and a green concrete moat filled with water circled all the way around the grounds. I walked past the castle part and followed the moat around to the far side, where I didn't see anyone. Since I was dressed as a bee I figured if I could sneak in I'd just look like someone who worked on the "Baby Bee" merry-go-round for toddlers. I glanced over my shoulder, then scooted on my rear down the side of the moat and slipped in. The water only came up to my knees but it was freezing cold, and the moat bottom was slippery with algae so I couldn't walk very quickly. I pushed one shoe forward, then the other. It was slow going and I got a little nervous. I twisted my bee body around and spotted a few people who had stopped to watch. This made me more nervous. I began to wave to them as if this were how I went to work every day—but then I lost my footing. My feet went straight up and I fell with a splash onto my back and I couldn't get up and soon the water was pouring through my bee ears.

"Help!" I hollered. "Help! I'm drowning."

Someone must have alerted the guards. In a few minutes two high school kids dressed in security uniforms scrambled down the bank and waded into the moat. They grabbed my arms and slowly pulled me upright, but it was hard to move me because my foam-and-fur bee costume had instantly sucked up about a million gallons of water. They couldn't drag me up the slippery side of the moat until four more guys pitched in to haul me out. I was the most unhappy soggy bee you've ever seen. I sat down on the curb and the water drained out of me and made a puddle as if I had *beed* my pants. One of the security guards offered to unzip me but that would have been worse.

Finally, an older guy approached me. I guess he was an undercover rent-a-cop at the park dressed like an Amish farmer. I could see that his goaty-looking beard was fake, but the badge he flashed was real.

"Don't be scared of me," he said, and pulled at a few long white hairs that were stuck to his lip.

"I'm not," I replied. "My dad's planning on buying this place." I was hoping they'd let me go if they thought I might soon be their boss.

"And when is your dad going to do that?" one of the young guys asked.

"As soon as he hits the mega lottery," I said.

All three of them laughed.

"So where does your dad live while he's planning his takeover of the theme park world?" the older cop asked with a sly smile.

"We own the Beehive Diner up the road," I said proudly, jerking my thumb in that direction, and as I looked up I saw a police car enter the parking lot with its lights flashing.

When the squad car pulled up next to us one of the security guards pulled me up onto my feet. From his window the cop saw how wet I was and frowned. "What's your name, kid?" he asked.

Without hesitating I replied, "Freddy Heinz." It

seemed so much easier to say it now that I was dressed like a bee.

"Well, Freddy," he continued, "I don't want my back-seat to get wet, so why don't you just promise me you won't pull a stunt like this again."

"I promise," I repeated.

"Okay, now buzz on back to the hive," he said, and laughed at his own joke as he drove off.

"Thanks for saving my life," I said, waving to the guys who pulled me out of the water, then I turned and sloshed across the parking lot. By the time I waddled all the way back to the diner Dad had returned with Mom.

"What happened to you?" she asked as I stood dripping and dejected in front of her. I looked like a stuffed animal that had gone through the washing machine.

"Don't go there," I replied. "Just help me out of here."

While she unzipped me Dad asked, "Did you drum up some good karma for the beehive?"

"Oh yeah," I said. "You got your ten bucks' worth of karma out of me."

"And I bet that FAST FOO trick got their attention," he said, proud of himself.

"It sure did," I replied. "In fact, I think you better put some FOO on the menu or people are going to be disappointed."

"Okay," he said, and rubbed his chin. "But what do you think FOO tastes like?" He gave Mom a puzzled look.

"Something kind of brown and sticky," I heard her say as I trudged back toward the house. When I got there I climbed up into my quiet room and sat on the bed in my wet underwear. I looked out the window and all the fall leaves were off the tree but one. It looked like a little hand sticking straight out and as I watched, a breeze came by and that last leaf fluttered but hung on. It seemed to need a helping hand. I hopped up and opened my window and reached for it. "Hang on, leaf friend," I said, "hang on. You can do it."

But it didn't. It let go. The leaf did not slowly drift to the ground where it could sadly look up and miss its twig and tree. No, once it let go it vanished in an instant and went from being something real to being something lost and blown away by a force it didn't understand.

Sitting there, I knew that soon Joey was going to blow away, too. I hadn't forgotten I'd told that cop I was Freddy Heinz, I just didn't want to think about what it meant. Maybe I was just trying to blame Freddy for all the trouble I got into at the park, but I knew it was more than that. "Give a camel an inch and he'll take a foot," I quietly said to myself. That much I understood.

8

GOT TO GIVE TO GET

It was Thanksgiving morning and I was practicing my daredevil skills when Mom heard me land hard and bounce onto the floor. Ever since my dive out the window, my balance has been lopsided. Normally I can run across the top rail of a fence or scamper up a rock-climbing wall without a problem. But now, when I jump down from my loft bedroom toward the living room couch, I have to make sure I land on the bean-bag chair I put on top the couch cushions. But even if I hit my target I sometimes bounce off and slam into the recliner or a side chair or something. Still, even if jumping is dangerous it's a lot quicker than climbing down the ladder.

"Is that you?" Mom called out from her bedroom when she heard the coffee table scrape across the floor.

"Nope," I yelled back. "It's Freddy."

"You fruit loop," she said. "Now come here."

I staggered into her room. I thought she was going to be mad so I smiled at her before she could frown at me.

But she was in a good mood. "If you are going to dive off the loft," she reminded me, "please wear your helmet. Okay?"

"Oops," I said touching my head. "Sorry."

"Well, you can make up for being scatterbrained by rubbing my legs," she continued. "They are so sore today. I had the same aches and pains when I was pregnant with you. This morning I got up for a little while and helped your dad at the diner but ran out of steam and now I'm just bushed."

"Dad can wear anyone out," I said. "He's like a weird cleaning machine."

I took a bottle of lotion from her bedside table and squeezed some into my hands to warm it up first.

"So," she said, trying not to sound pushy. "Have you given some thought to forgiving him? This is the perfect day to make it official."

"Can I get back to you on that?" I replied.

"Don't play games with me," she said sharply. "You have got to get over the past and move on. Now, I want you to stop making a drama out of this and do it."

"What if I don't feel like it?"

"Do you know how sad you have made me by not

embracing our new Heinz family life together?" she asked.

"I don't think this is something you can make me do," I said stubbornly.

"I don't think this is something you can defy me on," she replied.

I started to say something but she cut me off.

"You are speedy at everything in life. You zip around here like greased lightning. Your mind is moving a mile a minute. So I don't want you telling me that you need more time. Time is up. So you do what I told you to do. Forgive him in your heart and then when the time is right you forgive him to his face."

"Does that mean I have to be Freddy forever?" I asked.

"Look," she said harshly. "Get over the name issue. Freddy Heinz is a good name."

"For someone who really is Freddy Heinz," I said.

Her eyes popped open and she looked toward me and scowled. "Zip it up," she snapped. "You can argue with me till the cows come home, so just do as I say."

I sighed and rubbed her feet. "Well, I bet if he runs out of money he'll run out on us," I said spitefully, and looked at her to see what she'd say to that.

"You'll lose this bet just like you lost the last one," she said. "Because he needs love more than he needs money."

"Isn't that what he has you for?" I replied.

"No—that's what you are for, and little Heinzie, too," she said, rubbing her tummy. "There is nothing better than to be loved by your children and that's what he needs. Love in the form of forgiveness. Now get with it."

"Okay," I said. "I'll try."

"This isn't the kind of trying like you'll *try* to eat your vegetables, or *try* to eat squid," she insisted. "This is *do it*!"

"Do I have to?" I asked.

"Good Lord!" she cried out. "I could use a drink! When I was pregnant with you a little drink every now and again did me a world of good."

I stopped rubbing. "Don't say that," I said sadly. "It hurts my feelings."

"See," she responded. "No one likes hurt feelings. So forgive your father and let bygones be bygones. Let's get over this last big hurdle."

"Okay," I said in a small voice.

"Plus, it's Thanksgiving," she added. "Now get on out there and be thankful that he rescued us from that roach trap on Plum Street."

When I went into the diner kitchen Dad was already at work mixing up a small batch of gray-looking turkey burger meat in a metal bowl. He poured a measuring cup of oily brown sauce onto the mixture and stirred it with a large spoon.

"What are you doing?" I asked, and sniffed. Something smelled kind of fishy.

"Testing my secret sauce on the meat," he replied in a voice like a mad scientist. "I was thinking we might want to bottle it. You know, have a few items at the cash register for people to buy."

"What's it taste like?" I asked, reaching for the measuring cup, then pausing as I got close enough to get a good whiff.

"Stop!" he barked. "Don't taste it now. Let it soak in, and when I make a burger then you'll discover the magic in the meat."

"Fine with me," I agreed, and pulled away. "What can I do?"

"First, wash your hands, then open those gallon containers of cranberry sauce," he ordered, pointing to a stack of them. "Spoon it into paper cups and put them in the cooler."

"How much are you paying?" I asked, and stuck out my hand.

"This is a charity operation today," he said. "We are all volunteering. That's how you get good karma—through acts of goodwill."

"You told me you got it by meditating on the sound of one hand clapping," I replied.

He raised one hand in the air. "I'll show you what the sound of one hand clapping *feels* like," he said.

"It's bad karma to hit your kid," I shot back.

"Just get to work," he grumbled. "We are way behind."

I got busy with the cranberry sauce and then we shucked about a million ears of corn and scrubbed a mound of sweet potatoes, wrapped them in foil, and put them into our giant oven. By then Mom had revived in time to join us and mix up a batch of instant stuffing. While she did that, I cut up premade pumpkin pies and put pieces on paper dessert plates. After a couple hours of work we were beat.

"How about one of those famous turkey burgers?" Mom said. "I'm starving."

"Okay," he said. "The meat should have soaked up the sauce by now." He put one of his experimental burgers on the grill, and as it heated up a funky aroma filled the diner.

"That doesn't smell so fresh," she remarked. "Has the meat gone sour?"

"Hey," Dad replied, "it was discounted for a fast sale but no one is going to complain. Besides, when you get food for free you take what you're given. That's how life works. Beggars can't be choosers."

"Do you get good karma for serving up food poisoning?" she asked pointedly.

He ignored that. "Just wait until you taste this gourmet treat," he said, sliding the burger onto a bun and spooning a little of his secret sauce on top. "Then you'll change your tune. Now eat up."

Mom took a bite out of the burger and instantly spit it out into a paper towel. "You have to change this recipe," she sputtered. "Otherwise your customers are going to make a beeline right to the bathroom."

"Hey," he said, "don't insult my special sauce."

"Just stick with ketchup," she suggested. "It can hide the taste of dog food."

"Hey, buddy, you take a bite out of it," he instructed, sounding a bit exasperated. "Your mom is picking on me."

I was afraid. Just the smell of the sauce on that flattened grayish puck of turkey meat made my eyes water. "El Gordo! Quesadilla!" I called out to the dogs, who were also using the new names Dad gave them. "Come here." When it came to food they'd answer to any name we called them. They scampered over and I lowered the burger for them to eat. El Gordo instantly put on his brakes and did a reverse moon walk, and Quesadilla began to twitch as if she had permanent nerve damage.

"What does a dog know?" Dad asked. "They'll eat trash, then turn around and not eat what's good."

"Then *you* take a bite out of it," Mom suggested, daring him.

He held the burger with both hands and took a

huge bite as we leaned forward to watch him chew. "Best dang turkey burger I've ever eaten," he mumbled with his mouth churning.

"You really have become someone else," Mom remarked. "You've become the hungriest man on the planet."

Dad got up and opened a diet soda. He chewed and drank, chewed and drank until he had washed about half of it down. From the look on his face he couldn't take another bite.

"Okay, okay, *no más*," he said. "My special sauce isn't so special. Let's just stick to ketchup. After all, Heinz ketchup is part of my good karma past."

"Freddy," Mom said, taking control. "You take the rest of this failed experiment and practice cooking a burger while your dad and I make patties out of the rest."

"Before you go," he said to me, burping politely as he wiped his lips on a white kitchen towel, "and before all these people show up and we have to jump into action, I think we should have a family moment where we give thanks for what we have."

"Amen to that," Mom echoed.

Dad held his hands out and we all joined together.

"Freddy, you go first," Mom insisted, and when I glanced up at her she shot me that stern raised-eyebrow look.

I took a deep breath and looked down at the floor. I

waited for my heart to speak to me but my heart was too busy just keeping me alive, so I spoke what was on my mind. "I'm thankful that I'm with my family and that we are going to help other people," I said carefully, "because we've been helped so much in the past."

"Is that all?" Mom asked, raising her eyebrow again because I still hadn't said what she wanted me to say.

"Amen?" I guessed.

"Well, I have something to say," Dad eagerly cut in. "It's been burning a hole in me all day to say it." He closed his eyes and bowed his head. "I'm thankful I'm so blessed," he said solemnly. "I'm no longer drinking. I have my family back together again and now there is one more on the way."

When he stopped talking he peeked over at me. "Well? What do you think of that news? Huh? I've been dying to tell you."

"Well," I stammered, "I kind of already knew." I tilted my head toward Mom's rounded belly.

"Oh, I wanted it to be a surprise," he said, and looked disappointed.

"So, is it a boy or a girl?" I asked eagerly, wanting to cheer him up. "That would be a surprise."

"It's a Heinz!" Dad said proudly. "Either way, it's a quality product. And you know what else?" he added. "It won't know anything about our old family. It will have a fresh start—a clean slate. No bad Pigza karma raining on Heinzie's parade."

"What about me?" I asked. "Am I under a rain cloud of bad Pigza karma?"

"Hey, buddy," he said with sudden enthusiasm. "You can have sunny skies, too. All you have to do is switch over to the Heinz way of life and step into your future." He snapped his fingers. "It's as simple as one, two, three."

Just then a white van pulled into the parking lot. Dad's eyes bugged out and he looked at his watch.

"High noon!" he hollered. "Man your battle stations! I called every shelter in town. Man, we are going to have good karma for a *lifetime* if they all show up."

"Do you have the car keys?" Mom asked. "I need to go shopping for a few things."

"At a time like this?" Dad yelped, sounding both annoyed and panicky.

"Yes," she said calmly, "there are a lot of good car sales starting today and I think I should take advantage of the holiday deals. We're going to need a minivan for little Heinzie and all the baby stuff."

"But I need you to help," he pleaded. "This is a ton of work!"

"I won't be much help throwing up," she replied, rubbing her tummy and wrinkling up her entire face. "That secret icky sauce has done me in and who knows what it's doing to the baby."

"Okay." He sighed, reached into his pocket, and

tossed her the keys. "But take it easy on the sticker price."

"Don't worry," she said airily from over her shoulder as she marched off. "I've got a trade-in and a good-karma credit card."

Outside the front door a line of about a dozen men and women and some kids had gathered.

"Freddy," Dad commanded, "you start with the burgers but watch it because turkey meat cooks quickly, and I'll set up the buffet." He ran to the door to greet the arrivals and I got the grill going and began to deal out turkey burger patties like a pack of cards. From then on, I became a turkey-burger-making machine. Dad had everyone wait at the door for five minutes while he hustled back and forth between the kitchen and the coffee counter, where he set a tub of silverware and napkins, paper plates, and dishes of corn, sweet potatoes, stuffing, and cranberry sauce. He tossed me a plastic bag of sliced buns, and when the first burger was finished I flipped it into the air and caught it on the bottom of the bun. "Do you want fries with that?" I shouted loudly to no one in particular.

"Thanks for reminding me," Dad said as he dashed by. "I better turn on the Frialator 'cause some folks will want fries. And keep count of how many burgers you cook. That will be our lucky karma number."

We were lucky that the diner sat only twenty-eight

people at a time because we could hardly keep up with them. Dad kept running into the kitchen to get more food while people pitched in to help serve pie and coffee, clear tables, and wash extra silverware. Somehow it all worked out so that as one happy group finished up another hungry group took their place. Maybe Thanksgiving was the real secret sauce of life because no one complained about anything. If there was any such thing as good karma, then Dad was sure to get some. But even if there was no such thing as karma, it didn't matter because doing something to help other people was far better than receiving good luck—it was giving good luck to people who needed it.

And then something happened that confused me because it was good luck for someone, but bad luck for me. I was grilling burgers and I flipped one onto a bun and turned to serve it to the next person in line when in front of me a bouncy kid, who I thought I had seen before, was wearing a baseball jersey I had definitely seen before.

"Nice shirt," I said, and, just to make sure, I added, "Let me see the back."

He twisted his shoulders around.

PIGZA, it read. "Nice name," I remarked, and felt kinda dead inside.

"Not my name," he replied. "My dad gave it to me."

I wanted to say, "My dad took it away from me," but

I didn't and instead I got all worked up and shouted, "Do you want fries with that?"

"Sure," he said. "I love fries."

"Me too," I replied, "but it'll take a few minutes."

"Okay," he said, "and bring some more ketchup to the table. I love ketchup. Lots and lots of ketchup. Like a really big bottle of ketchup."

"Yeah," I said. I quickly went into the back freezer and pulled out a bag of precut fries and tossed an order into the Frialator. When I returned to the grill Dad was serving burgers to the retired war vets waiting in line.

"Where'd you run off to?" he snapped.

"Bathroom," I replied innocently. "And I washed my hands."

"Well don't abandon your post again!" he ordered as he tossed me the spatula and dashed off to clear dirty dishes from a table as a new family waited to take a seat.

I made a few more burgers and got them started, then ran back to check on the fries. They were golden brown so I dumped them onto a plate and grabbed a fresh bottle of ketchup from behind the counter.

"Here you go," I said to the kid, and set the plate on the table. He was sitting with his mom and two younger twin boys. They must have been brothers because all three were equally skinny and fidgety and had the same baldy haircuts.

"Thanks," he said, and right away began slapping the bottom of the ketchup bottle with his open palm. When that didn't loosen it up he began pounding the bottle on the table top, which is what I always do, and suddenly I realized he was the kid I had seen at the school who had to sit in the big time-out chair just as I had to do when I was in special ed. It was like looking at my old troubled past again, where I was constantly punished, and it made me like the kid right away even though he was now pounding the bottle on the table so hard that the silverware jangled and water sloshed out of glasses and people turned in their seats to glare at him as he grunted like a pig each time he slammed the bottle down.

"Hey!" his mom hollered, as she wrestled with the two other boys, who were sword fighting with their finished ears of corn. "Cut it out!"

He stopped pounding the bottle on the table and returned to smacking it with his open hand.

I knew I had to get back to the grill or Dad would growl at me but I just couldn't take my eyes off that kid. In some odd way I felt like I had become Freddy and I was watching a movie of Joey in action and before I could snap out of it the kid smacked the bottle just right and the ketchup blasted out the opening and hit his plate with a loud splat and sprayed onto everyone at the table.

"Awesome!" yelled one of the twins, pointing at my face. "You look dead!"

A dollop of ketchup had hit me in the forehead and was running down my nose.

"My turn," the other one said, and they wrestled for the bottle.

The mom lurched forward and reached for the ketchup but was blasted again before she finally snatched the dripping bottle from the kid.

That killed the conversation and I ran off to get them some towels. When I returned she was in the bathroom.

"Sorry," the kid said, licking the ketchup from his arm as if he were a cat.

"Don't worry," I replied. "You want a clean shirt?"

"No way," he said, "this one tastes good." He shoved a spot into his mouth and sucked on it.

"Freddy!" Dad hollered. "Get over here."

I could smell turkey burning. "See you around," I said to the kid and hustled back to the grill.

"I thought I told you not to get lost," Dad snarled.

"Sorry," I replied, and began to flip the burnt burgers into the trash.

"Faster!" he ordered. "Bee-sting fast!"

"Stop it with the *bee* stuff," I said. "I'm buzzing around as fast as I can."

"I think that med patch is slowing you down,"

he growled, and his arm jerked toward my shoulder.

"Don't mess with me," I shot back, and raised the spatula.

From across the room one of the twins yelled out, "Duck!" as the ketchup bottle came twirling end over end through the air and hit Dad so hard on the back of his head with a loud thunk that I thought he was going to die. His knees buckled, but he didn't go down. His eyes looked like two shooting stars as he braced himself against the counter. After a moment of standing very still he gathered his strength up and looked mighty angry when he turned, pointed to the kids, and savagely shouted, "You three rascals! Outside! Now!"

"He did it," the twins said, pointing at their older brother as they scampered for the door.

"I'm innocent!" the kid with the jersey said, and made a dash for the spinning bottle. But he couldn't quite reach it because at that moment his mom stepped out of the bathroom and as he bent over she hooked a finger through his back belt loop and dragged him toward the exit while she called out an apology to Dad.

"I'm innocent!" the kid protested as he swung back and forth, and then once he was beyond the door I could still hear him crying out, "I'm innocent! I'm innocent!" until he was closed up in a van with the others.

Right after that the mood in the diner changed and

everyone seemed to finish their meals at once. Dad just sat on a stool with his shoulders sagging down and his head in his hands. I stood by the front door and as everyone filed past I said, "Happy Thanksgiving from the Beehive," and I gave them a ten-percent-off coupon for our Grand Opening, whenever that was. When the last person was gone I quickly flicked off the lights and hung the CLOSED sign in the front window.

"My head is killing me," Dad moaned.

"Now you know how I felt," I said.

I got some ice from the freezer and wrapped it in a dish towel and brought it to him.

He held it against the back of his head. "I hope that flying bottle didn't undo all the good karma we earned," he sighed, sounding worried.

"I don't think so," I said. "It was an accident."

"Maybe," he speculated. "But everything happens for a reason."

"You'll know for sure if it was good or bad when you play the lottery," I said, and rested the side of my face on the table. I was exhausted.

"How many burgers did you serve?" he asked.

"I counted a hundred and thirty-seven," I replied, guessing a bit.

"Make that one hundred and thirty-eight," he added as he turned on a hanging lamp and plucked a pen from his pocket.

"What do you mean?" I asked.

"Dick came to the back door and I gave him a burger while you were chatting with those wild kids," he explained.

"Why didn't he come in?" I asked.

" 'Cause he stole from me," he said harshly. "After the rewedding I loaned him some money and he never paid me back, so he's not exactly welcome."

"But if you forgive him that would be good karma," I pointed out.

"Today's karma was about food," he said bluntly. "If he wants forgiveness I told him to come back with the cash."

Even though I was tired I knew that wasn't true. Dad could pay me all he wanted but he couldn't buy forgiveness. That came from the heart.

"You should be nicer to him," I whispered. "He made a mistake. We all do."

Dad reached over and put his hand on my head. "You're right," he said, stroking my hair. "I'm just mad at him. But I'll get over it and we'll work it out."

"That'll bring you mega karma," I whispered with my voice trailing off. I closed my eyes, and the last thing I remember was Dad's frantic scratching on a piece of paper as he mumbled numbers to himself. "Two hundred ears of corn . . . a hundred and fifty sweet potatoes . . . ten gallons of cranberry sauce . . ."

I don't know how much time had passed, but I was asleep when Mom drove up in her new minivan and honked the horn. I opened my eyes and Dad was still working on his numbers.

"Can we clean up tomorrow?" I asked, yawning.

"Better than that," he replied, and tapped on his list of numbers. "Once I play these winners I think I'll just have this diner towed away. It will be a lot easier to junk it than clean it. Besides," he said, looking around, "I don't know how much more of this cleaning and cooking I can take."

We went out to inspect Mom's new minivan, which was bright yellow with a black interior. "Anyone want to buzz off for dinner?" Mom asked. "I'll treat."

We piled in and drove to the Chinese Dragon Buffet, but instead of eating inside the restaurant we got the food to go and sat in the minivan and smelled the new car smell while we watched a movie on the minivan's DVD player. That was the best Thanksgiving dinner I'd ever had.

9

GRANNY'S COMET

I had been collecting cigarette butts for some time because I was looking forward to visiting my grandmother's grave. She died a year ago after fifty years of smoking what she figured was fifty thousand packs of cigarettes, enough that if you stacked the cigarettes end to end you would have a cigarette tower over sixty-eight miles high so that if you climbed up and sat on top of it you would actually be in outer space breathing from a tank of oxygen—and that's how she ended her life, breathing out of a tank of oxygen, but instead of being in outer space looking down at me she is underground looking up at me. Still, I'd rather have her here on earth than have to search the universe through a telescope as if she were a comet exhaling a little trail of cigarette smoke across the starry sky. Once, I was watching TV and they showed an aerial view of a forest fire raging out of control on either side of a highway and I yelled toward the kitchen where she was cooking, "Come here quick and see what your lungs look like!"

She glanced at the flames on the TV then glared down at me. "That's what your bottom is going to feel like when I smack you with this frying pan."

She never took criticism well, but I loved her and wanted to do something special, so that's why I collected the cigarette butts and bottle caps and bits of foil plus I had found a spray can of silver paint in the diner tool closet. I figured it might work like spray-on tinsel so I added it to my bag of supplies, which also included a big tube of Super Glue.

It was sad that Granny was dead but I was happy with my tombstone plan as I walked the few miles from the diner down highway 30 toward St. Mary's Cemetery, which was right behind our old house where I had hit my head.

Tall Amish buggies clip-clopped by me like wooden outhouses on wagon wheels. I waved to the people sitting bundled up inside and they waved and smiled back, which was nice because I had a huge wool knit Christmas cap stretched down over my ears so my head was the shape of an enormous acorn. They could have pointed and laughed at me but they didn't because they were Amish, which meant they were always polite. Although the other day Dad pointed at some

Amish kids downtown who were staring at a really fancy car. "The young ones can't always live up to be-ing Amish," he said. "There is a bunch of them that have secret apartments and cars and go out drinking and looking for non-Amish girlfriends. You can be trapped inside your own skin and sometimes you just want to rip it off and be someone different."

Even though he was talking about them, I knew he was really talking about himself. He always seemed to be two people at once and I wasn't sure why. But maybe it was like Mom had said, with forgiveness you can breathe easy inside your own skin. Without it, you are always trying to be someone else.

A line of cars had gotten stuck behind the slow-moving Amish buggies that clogged up the road. The car drivers kept gassing their vehicles forward then falling back, then lurching forward again, then back. I waved to them, too, but they didn't look very happy. They wanted to speed up and leave me far behind and that reminded me of Charles, who wanted me to leave Joey behind at the speed of light. But becoming Freddy wasn't so easy, and it was just going to take one step at a time like the steady clip-clop trotting of the horses. That is one reason I was looking forward to sitting by Granny's grave and having a private chat with her. It had been a long time since I heard her voice in my mind, and with all the pressure on me to "forgive and forget" I thought she would come up with some good advice.

Dad had given me some time off even though it had been a week after Thanksgiving and I had cleaned every square inch of the diner. The dogs were still prowling through the outside trash bins for scraps and El Gordo even got his paw stuck in the ketchup bottle that smacked Dad's head. I had to pour cooking oil around the opening to wiggle his leg out. The only place it was messy was around Dad's desk. The floor was littered with ripped-up mega-lottery tickets and loser scratch cards. Each time the kitchen door swung open the paper fluttered up like spooked butterflies then settled down again.

"Are we ever going to have our grand opening?" I asked him one morning after a couple days of doing nothing but watching the Home Shopping Network with Mom and waiting for the mail to deliver her purchases.

"That plan is on hold," he said in a distracted voice as he punched numbers into his calculator. "I could work in this diner forever and not make a pot of beans, or I could put my energy into the lottery and make a pot of gold. And believe me, I'd rather go for the gold!"

"So, how is the gold stacking up?" I asked, thinking that the more *he* had the more *we* had.

"Well, after I earned all that good karma," he said proudly, "I played a combination of the number of people we served with the date that Mom says the doctor gave us for Heinzie's birth. But they were all losers."

For a moment the expression on his face was so sad I had to look away.

"But it was my fault," he said, perking up. "I had been thinking too small and only hoping for a regular payoff. Now I figure once I start aiming for the mega jackpot and get a winner, then we can retire in style for the rest of our lives."

"Can we retire to Disney World?" I asked. "I'd really love to live in Snow White's castle and be the eighth dwarf. You could call me Zippy, the dwarf who gets things done."

"I'm thinking more about a castle in Miami Beach," he said firmly, "where you would be Freddy the houseboy and call me Sir Charles and do everything I tell you to do."

"What's a houseboy?" I asked.

"A boy who won't leave the house and go play with his imaginary friends," he said, sounding unhappy with me.

"Am I bugging you?" I asked because his patience seemed a bit thin. "If I am on your nerves maybe I can just disappear?"

"Help yourself," he said without a fuss. "There is

nothing to do around here unless you want to snake out the toilet. The place is beginning to smell."

"I already cleaned it yesterday," I said.

"Well, this morning I was flushing down a bag of lottery scratch tickets and it got stopped up," he said, and shrugged.

"How much are you paying?" I asked.

"Your next meal," he replied abruptly, definitely not sounding like he had a pot of gold.

"Do *I* want fries with that?" I shouted to the shiny funhouse image of myself in the chrome paneling. "Why, yes *I* do!" I replied just as loudly. "Golden fries!"

"By the time I count to three," he threatened, holding up three fingers. "One, two . . ." But then he quickly lowered his hand and buttoned his lip because Mom showed up.

"Hi, boys," she said, smiling widely as she pushed through the swinging kitchen door. The lottery tickets swirled about her legs as she spun in a circle like a freshly perfumed fashion model. "How do you like my new maternity outfit?" She had on a pair of turquoise stretch pants and a fluffy pink sweater, which was short-waisted and exposed her swollen belly.

"Can you pull your sweater down?" I asked. "Everyone can see the tattoo around your belly button." I never liked the lacey red words circling the rim of her belly button: *Press here for more options*. Last year she ordered me to do my homework and I gave her belly button a good poke and squawked, "What's my next option?" In about two seconds I was locked in my bedroom *with* my homework.

"I happen to think this is a good look for me," she said, tugging her sweater back down as she gave me a cross look.

Then she turned to Dad. "What's your opinion?" she asked.

"You are my *especial fashionista*," he exclaimed with his big eyes flashing up at her. "Now, come here," he said sweetly, "and let me rub your tummy for good luck. Maybe you'll be my Aladdin's lamp and little Heinzie will pop out of your mouth like a genie and grant me three wishes."

"Well, if that happens," Mom said, adjusting her hair with nails that were shaped like pink hearts, "he'll be *my* genie and those wishes will get *me* out of this"—she waved around at the diner as she searched for the right words—"this tin hot dog."

"Let me rub your belly for luck anyway," Dad cooed, "and I'll send Joey out to buy a lottery ticket for tonight's drawing."

She inched forward on her high heels, and as soon as his open hand touched her belly he jerked back with a sudden inspiration. "Mercy!" he shouted as he slapped at the table for a scrap of paper, and with his eyes closed he furiously wrote down a string of numbers. When he opened his eyes he held up the paper and gave it a kiss. "The jolt I got just now," he announced to us, "is exactly the same feeling I had when I won the big money that changed my life."

"You'd better be right," Mom said with a straight face, "otherwise you are acting pretty weird."

Dad folded the little piece of paper up in a ten-dollar bill then leaned forward and seized my open hand by the wrist. As he closed my fingers over the paper ball he sang to Mom, "He's got the tiny little baby in his hands, he's got you and me baby in his hands, he's got the whole world in his hands."

I smiled. Granny always sang me that song when we curled up on the couch and took a nap together.

"Now don't forget to buy that ticket with those exact numbers," Dad reminded me. "In your hands could be the front door key to our new castle."

"Yes, don't forget," Mom echoed as she picked dog hair off her sweater.

"Don't worry," I promised them, heading over to the house to get dressed. "I've got the whole world in my hands."

As I walked down the highway toward the cemetery I kept feeling for the little paper that Dad had written his numbers on. My fingers sorted through the cigarette butts and bottle caps and crinkly candy wrappers in my pocket until I felt the ten-dollar bill all folded up in a tight square.

Just before I reached the cemetery I passed by the neighborhood discount store and saw a stack of boxes. There was a big one that had been used to pack plastic Santas you could plug in and light up in your yard. The wind had been blowing harder and I figured the cemetery would be cold, so I grabbed the box and carried it over my head like an upside-down canoe.

By the time I got to Granny's grave the sky was overcast and I thought it might snow. Her stone was easy to find because it was a red granite stone another family had ordered for some other dead person but then they never picked it up. Who knows what happened? But because it had someone else's name on it we could buy it at a "used" discount. The tombstone store chiseled off the old name and then flipped the stone around and carved PETUNIA ROSE PIGZA on the reverse side. I didn't even know that was her full name until I first saw the stone. I only knew her as Granny Pigza.

I dropped the box down over the tombstone and climbed under. It was less windy but dark. I found a sharp rock and scratched on the cardboard until I carved out a small window. That's when I discovered Dad had visited, too. He had taken some metal tool and scratched lines over Granny's real name and had roughly etched in ELIZABETH PATRICIA HEINZ. I imagined Granny looking up through that stone as if it were her periscope on the world, and it was as if he had scratched her eyes out. I just hoped he hadn't dug up her jar of ashes and transferred them into a ketchup bottle.

With my gloved hands I rubbed the stone up and down and knocked off all the bird mess and dirt that was stuck to it. Even though she was a few feet under the ground I felt we were connected. She was born a Pigza and died a Pigza. "You'll always be the same Granny to me," I said with my hands on either side of the stone as if I were holding her by the shoulders. "And I'll always be Joey to you."

Then I got to work. First I used spit and dirt to make cement and smoothed out the scratches Dad made. Then I pulled out all the supplies from my pockets and made a pile of cigarette butts, bottle caps, and colorful paper. I held the can of spray paint inside my jacket to keep it warm and took out the tube of glue.

"Someday," I said to her, "I'm going to be buried next to you, jar to jar. You never ran off. You never changed who you were. You were always proud of yourself no matter what."

Already I felt better. Talking to her was almost like old times except she wasn't telling me to shut up like she did even when I was saying sweet things to her. I began to glue the cigarette butts end to end until I had the outline of a Christmas tree. Then I glued bottle caps on the tips of the branches, and folded up a red foil candy wrapper into a star for the top. It started to look pretty good but not as good as the tree Granny and I dragged home a few years ago. We got it for free because it was the night before Christmas and the tree sellers allowed anyone to have what was left in their parking lot. We didn't have much to decorate it with because she had stored the tree decorations in a place she couldn't remember. But then she had a stroke of genius. Since we had a dozen honey-glazed doughnuts we bought for Christmas morning breakfast, we stuck those on the branches. That was such a good idea that we raided the kitchen for other food we could turn into ornaments.

"We'll have a few rules," she insisted. "Nothing that will rot and smell, like sardines or strips of bacon."

"Darn," I said, and put the sardines back in the cupboard.

"No baloney," she said.

"But Swiss cheese would work," I pointed out, "because of the holes."

"Okay," she said hesitantly. "As long as you eat it in the morning with the doughnuts."

That sounded good to me. She hung dry egg noodles on the ends of branches like curly icicles. In the back of a cupboard I found a baggie full of Cheerios that Granny said must have been "nasty old" because she used to bag them up for me to snack on when I was a toddler. She dug out some fuzzy LifeSavers from the bottom of her purse and I uncovered a tin of stale hot-mustard pretzels above the refrigerator. Granny topped it off with some balls of aluminum foil and pressed some gummy bears onto the sharp pine needles. When we were finished it wasn't too bad-looking, and on Christmas morning we had plenty to pick and eat as we opened our presents, although the Swiss cheese got stiff and curled up.

I finished decorating the tombstone with the spray paint. I pushed the box off so I could breathe and sprayed the decorations and the whole stone silver. It looked really beautiful. Then I pulled the box back down. Finally I reached into a secret zipper pocket inside my jacket and pulled out a small package. "Here is your Christmas gift," I said, and placed it under the tree. It was an almost-full pack of real cigarettes I'd found in Dad's dresser. I wanted to get her the chewing gum he used that helps you to stop smoking, but since she was already dead I thought she might as well get what she really wanted.

She always did the same for me. Each year Granny gave me a piece of paper and told me to write down what it was that I wanted for Christmas. "Just one thing," she insisted. "You might luck out and get more than one, but you are not allowed to be greedy because some kids get none—so one is all you should expect."

And each year I wrote down just one thing and it always turned up under the tree, just as she said it would. This year all I wanted from her was advice. I pulled a little paper out of my pocket.

"I only have one thing on my list," I said. I opened it up and read, "Should I forgive him?" Then I folded the piece of paper up and tucked it under her gift.

"What do you think of that?" I said out loud. "I think that if I do it he'll have all the power because then he won't need me for anything else. What do you think?"

And then it was as if her voice rose up in me and I could hear her. "You got it all backwards," she said in that smoky, harsh voice of hers. "He'll get tired of waiting for you to forgive him and after a while he won't care what you do. But if you forgive him, then it will put you in control. Think about it," she said. "Who is the bigger person? The one who can forgive or the one who can't?"

Just that one thought felt like a new beginning. She was right. It always made you stronger to be the "bigger" person.

"I have to go now," I said to her. I leaned forward and gave the stone a kiss. It was as cold as the last time I kissed her cheek. "I miss you," I said quietly. "I'm sorry all that smoking did you in. But I guess we have that in common, too, because now I have to send Joey up in smoke and become that other kid."

When I crawled out from under the box the weather had changed. It was spitting snow. I looked across the cemetery at all the gloomy, slump-shouldered tombstones. It didn't seem right how the living made the dead look so defeated. Just because a person's life was over didn't mean they ever regretted being alive.

For a moment I stood there like a revved-up car out of gear. This was one of those moments when I wished I was my old hyper self again and could go darting between the stones as if outrunning my thoughts. Now I try to think everything through, and when I can't seem to find answers to what I want to do next, or say next, or even think next, I feel just as dumb and dead inside as one more cold stone. That's how I felt with the snow coming down. All my thoughts looked as if they were nothing but silent dots of snow falling from the sky.

I turned and looked one more time at Granny's holiday stone. She may have been dead but her memory was alive. "Merry Christmas," I said in a voice cheerful enough to make both of us feel better. "You are my tombstone *fashionista*!"

Then my gears began to shift and slowly I turned and walked away, pulling the box behind me until I came to the fence behind our old house where I dropped it. Through the curtained windows I could see moving shadows of the new renters inside. To me they looked like shadow puppets of our old selves and

I tried to imagine what they might be saying, but the conversations between Mom and Dad didn't always make me feel good so I just left.

I went out the cemetery gate and walked over to the Turkey Hill Mini Mart. As soon as I walked in I began to laugh because there was a display of Heinz ketchup. "Hi, brother," I said to a bottle, and slapped it a high five. I knocked it off the shelf and had to catch it before it hit the floor. After I put it back I settled down and gave the cashier the ten dollars and a piece of paper with the numbers Dad wanted to play.

"You have to be eighteen to play the lottery," he said, pointing to a sign next to the machine.

"I am eighteen," I said. "My growth is stunted because of my mom and dad."

"I hear you," he said, and smiled. Then he took my money and punched in the numbers.

When the cashier handed me the tickets I shoved them into my pocket. Buying the tickets was the last thing I had to do but I really didn't want to go home.

For a while I just walked around the neighborhood, passing all the places where I grew up and knew so well. It was pretty clear to me that I was someplace between leaving Joey behind, forgiving Carter, and becoming Freddy—but I didn't know where that place was until I walked back along highway 30 and returned to the diner. I stood there and looked at it, trying to imagine how it would look when Dad finally got around to getting a proper sign and giving it the bee-color paint job. The lights were off. Snow had gathered along the top like the white on a skunk's tail. And then I walked right up to the back side of it and pulled out my spray can and with the little bit left inside I just managed to write out, *I AM NOT JOEY PIGZA.*

The last dying hiss of the spray can was like the air going out of Joey. I guess that was his last gasp.

10

PAINT-BY-NUMBERS CHRISTMAS

After putting Joey into hibernation, I woke up each morning and made up who I was. I opened my eyelids and imagined my eyeballs flashing wildly in my head like tumbling lotto numbers, and when they stopped my best qualities might have won out and I could rise out of bed like the sweetest boy in the world, or my worst qualities might have gotten lucky and turned me into a crazy kid who banged around the house like a chicken with its head cut off just as Granny said. It was hard to tell who I'd be until I got going, and the best part was that no matter what happened, it was Freddy who was responsible. Joey was definitely off the hook.

On Christmas morning it was no different. I opened my eyes and just felt the good kid in me had hit his numbers. I had that winning feeling running through my body. I woke up before Mom and Dad, but instead of jumping from my loft I quietly slinked down my ladder without sneaking a look toward the predecorated Christmas tree Mom had bought at a United Way fundraiser. Since Dad and I had thrown away all our old Pigza tree decorations, Mom said she was now building "the new Heinz Family collection of keepsakes." I slipped outside and trotted through the frosty air over to the diner. "Freddy is very quiet today," I whispered to myself.

Out in the diner I got the griddle turned up and started the coffee then mixed up a batch of pancake batter. I put the bacon on and poured the maple syrup into a stainless pitcher and heated it up. "Freddy is a very organized fellow," I said with my chin held high.

I set out two trays for the platters of food and coffee cups and plates and utensils and napkins. Then it occurred to me, "Freddy is forgetting the little four-legged creatures." I tossed a couple of hot dogs on the griddle for El Gordo and Quesadilla. "So far, so good," I said to myself.

Once I had the pancakes made and everything ready, it took me two trips to carry the trays across to the dining room in the house. By then Mom was up and had plugged in the thousands of sparkling white star lights so that the tree glittered as if it were dipped in diamond dust. She was sorting gifts and doing some final arranging around the tree as she hummed along with a tiny musical ornament that played "Jingle Bells."

"Merry Christmas!" I yelled over at her.

She turned and smiled back. "Merry Christmas to you, sweetie," she sang, and from that perfect moment on it was as if we were living out some happy-family Christmas play where we all knew our parts by heart.

"I have breakfast," I announced, pointing to the trays. "See?"

"Freddy, you are an angel. Get me a cup of coffee and I'll wake Charles up," she said. "But no peeking, okay?"

"Okay," I said as joyfully as one of Santa's helpers, then began to pick up the tune from "Jingle Bells" while I set the table.

It didn't take long for Dad to join us. He looked a little tired, as if he'd been up all night cleaning each little light on the tree while counting them for some lottery-number scheme. "Did Santa visit?" he asked, tying his robe around his waist. At that moment we all locked eyes onto the tree. Santa had been *very* generous. There were packages stacked up as tall and wide as the Great Wall of China, and nailed onto the old barn beam over the window were three long red stockings, each one looking as full and lumpy as a snake that had swallowed a zoo.

"Wow," I said. "What a haul."

"Looks like Santa didn't save anything for other people," Dad remarked.

"Santa went on a shopping spree," Mom said, perky and full of joy. "Santa was having a very good year!"

"Freddy, bring the trays over by the tree," Dad suggested. "We'll eat under the stars and rip open some gifts."

We did just that. First we started with the stockings. I got a pair of fuzzy slippers and a new wallet for all the money I was going to make, and a cookbook on how to whip up world-famous diner food and another book titled *Homeschooling for Dummies*. Dad got a crystal ball that you stared into and it magically revealed answers to your questions, and he got a set of tarot cards to predict the future and a guide to palm reading with one free palm-reading session with a real Gypsy. Mom got a carved monkey-paw back scratcher, a pair of noise-blocking headphones, and lots of skin-toning lotion. We took a break to eat and then, at Mom's request, we started working through that solid wall of gifts from her and Santa.

Out of soft packages and hard boxes came shoes, socks, underwear, T-shirts, belts, pants, shirts, sweaters, jackets, coats, gloves, hats, scarves, handkerchiefs, and more. At first it was fun to imagine wearing all new things but then it seemed odd because Mom got me and Dad the exact same things. The colors, the brands, the styles were exactly alike. Freddy didn't know what to say. Dad was smiling from ear to ear, and then Mom said, "You two boys have so much in common."

"Yes we do," Dad and Freddy said at the same time.

"But more than just clothes," she said. "There are toys."

She walked me to the window on the far side of the house and put her hands over my eyes. "I couldn't get you the motor scooter you asked for," she said. "But I hope this does the trick."

When she removed her hands I was staring out at an all-terrain vehicle. In fact, I was staring at *two* awesome ATV's—one red and one black. But before I could run out of the house and jump onto one of them and chew up the turf, she grabbed me by the neck. "There are rules," she stressed.

At that moment Dad whipped open the coat closet, grabbed something that I thought was a bowling ball, then turned toward me with a big black-and-yellow helmet. On the back of it was stenciled NUMBER ONE WORKER BEE.

"You have to wear this," he said. "For your own safety. If just once you don't wear it, I'll take away the ATV and that will be the end of it."

I looked at the helmet. I could see Freddy Heinz's goofy face reflected on the polished stripes and it felt to me like his eyes were spinning around like a winner. "Okay," I agreed. "Not a problem."

Then Dad went back to the closet and pulled out his own helmet, which read in stenciled letters KING BEE. "Plus," he said, grinning widely, "there is more."

There was. I attacked a stack of boxes that he carried out from the closet. I got a paintball gun with a supply of power cartridges and a box of two thousand orange paintballs. I got a neck protector and face mask and a full-body camouflage outfit along with army boots, and knee and elbow pads. "Freddy is very pleased," I whispered to myself as my trigger finger twitched.

Dad opened his extra boxes and he got what I got, except his paintballs were yellow. I glanced over at Mom and she smiled knowingly. "Like father, like son," she said with a twinkle in her eye.

"Freddy is the happiest boy on the planet," I said to her. And deep inside I was happy. Very, very happy. And very, very eager to get going. But I couldn't cut loose just yet. The happy Christmas play wasn't over.

Once Dad and I finished opening all our paintball equipment he announced that it was his turn to give some gifts. This time he got Mom exactly what she wanted. When she opened the little jewelry box with the big diamond ring, the tears ran down her cheeks and she stood up and gave him a big kiss and hug.

"I guess it's hard to wear that diner on your finger," he said slyly as he reached for her hand. "Pretty silly of me to think it would make a great wedding present."

"You are a fast learner," she replied, and slipped the ring on.

It was big. "Impressive," she said, and held her limp hand out. "You may kiss the Queen Bee's ring," she ordered.

Charles dropped down on one knee and gave it a kiss.

When it was my turn I gave her a kiss, and an envelope. She opened it up. It was a brochure from a company that removed tattoos by laser.

"They offer a free appointment right downtown," I said. "And then I promise you I will work and save up enough money to have that belly button tattoo removed."

"That is very thoughtful," she said. "But I like my tattoo."

"Well, think about it," I asked. "I called and they won't do anything until you have the baby." And before she could say anything else I gave her a big box. It was one of those baby spy cameras that you can clip on to your baby's crib and watch it sleep on a little screen you can keep with you while you are in another room doing other stuff.

"Oh, I love this," she said. "It's just what I wanted."

"There is only one channel," I said. "All little Heinzie all the time."

"Do you think I can get reception at the mall?" she asked. "It would be super great if I could see when he wakes up and then run home."

"We'll test it out later," Charles said as I tossed the dogs chew toys in the shape of burritos.

After every gift was handed out and we were all slumped down as if we had eaten a fifty-course meal, I pointed at a low branch on the tree. "There is one more," I said. Charles and Maria exchanged a glance. I ducked under the tree and grabbed it, then wriggled back out.

I looked at the tag. "Why, it's for you, Charles," I sang and handed him the flat package which was about the size of a postage stamp and weighed about the same.

As he unknotted the thin ribbon and peeled tape from the folded paper, I could feel my heart unwrapping. *This is it*, I said to myself. *This is really it. Get ready, Freddy.*

When he had completely unfolded the paper wrapping, he looked baffled and then turned the paper upside down. Then right side up. He searched his lap and around his feet. A very alarmed look crossed his face. "I can't seem to find what it was you gave me," he said as if he had already lost it.

"That's because it's an invisible gift," I replied. "You can't see it, but it's the biggest thing in the room."

He looked confused. "Is this a puzzle I'm supposed to figure out?" he asked.

"It's actually a puzzle that *other* boy had to figure out first," I said. "Your Christmas gift is actually the answer to the puzzle. Are you ready?"

He nodded. "Bring it on," he said.

I looked him right in the eye, and I wasn't faking it when I said, "Freddy forgives you. He forgives you for everything. All of it. Even stuff he doesn't know about. Even stuff he hasn't even imagined."

He started to say something but I held up a finger and stopped him.

"And," I said, "from now on I'm Freddy Heinz plain and simple. That other kid, what's-his-name, has left the building."

"I hate to burst your bubble," he said, and cocked his hands on his hips, "but Charles Heinz hasn't done *anything* that needs forgiving."

I didn't know what to say and for a blank moment I felt as if I was neither Joey nor Freddy. I looked at Mom as if she'd stabbed me in the back, but she looked just as shocked.

"You know me—I'm just joking," he said quickly, and opened his arms wide as he stooped down and smiled his wide goofy smile. "Now come here and give me a hug, Freddy me boy!"

I guess something in me really wanted to be hugged by Charles or Carter or Dad or whatever his name was, and in return I wanted to love him and be loved by him and feel that huge sigh of relief which comes with everything finally being normal and perfect. The power of that forgiveness swept through me, and all my old worries about him vanished and I sprang forward and wrapped my arms around his neck.

"What took you so long to stop being a jerk?" I asked, squeezing him tightly.

"I don't know," he said, pulling me away from his neck so he could look into my face. His eyes were shiny with tears, which made the tears stream down my face. "But for sure I didn't realize how good it feels to be a family man. Now put your arms around me and let me get caught up on a decade of hugs."

"And what about me?" I asked. "I need some hugs, too."

"Every man for himself," he cried out, gripping my wrists tightly as he stood and swung me around so suddenly my feet left the ground, and as he spun and turned I was spinning straight out like the spokes on a wheel until I realized I wasn't so much hugging him as I was just barely hanging on.

"You are so weird!" I howled as I circled around.

"I know," he howled back. "But keep it a secret."

"Too late for that," I yelled back.

Then he started to laugh and as he did he lost his

footing and began to stumble and I began to wobble and suddenly he tripped over a pile of paper and boxes and as he staggered and fell he let go of me and I went flying up over the little plastic tree we decorated just for the dogs and landed with a full-body slam across the leather couch cushions.

My skin was stinging but I hopped up and shouted, "Are you okay?" He was, because he was all rolled up in the wrapping paper and laughing.

"Is it possible," he said as he pushed himself up off the floor, "is it possible that I'm becoming more like you?"

"Do you want fries with that?" I asked.

"Yes," he said, "I do want fries with that." Then he rubbed his backside. "Oh, I think I bruised my bottom but it reminded me of one more gift." He pulled out his wallet, flipped it open, and removed a Pennsylvania State Identification Card. "I've been saving it for you," he said.

I looked at it. There was my picture. Beneath it was FREDDY HEINZ and my birth date and our new address.

"It's official," I said, and showed it to Mom.

"Well, now that you two have your *guy issues* worked out, why don't you go outside and do what guys do best," she suggested.

I gave her a puzzled look.

"You know what I mean," she said. "Now take your guns and go shoot each other."

"Come on," I yelled at Dad. "It's time to play with our toys!"

At that moment the Christmas play was over and another play began. We both got suited up in our paintball outfits and went outside with our guns slung over one shoulder and ammo bags over the other.

"I get the black ATV," I called out, quickly hopping up onto the seat.

"We should make a few rules," he said.

"Why?" I asked. "Here is what I think. We just ride around and shoot at each other."

"But just in the farm fields out back," he said.

"Can we go on the highway?" I asked.

"No!" he said sharply.

"Darn," I said. I really wanted to take a shot at that little clown car.

I turned the key on my ATV and it fired right up. I had never driven one before but it looked easy.

"You just turn the throttle like a motorcycle," Dad instructed. "There's a front brake on the left handgrip and a back brake on the foot pedal."

I revved my engine. It was like Freddy had been doing it all his life. "Every man for himself!" I hollered, then I began to fill the auto feed tank on the paint gun. It could fire a hundred and fifty shots, each as fast as I pulled the trigger. His would do the same, but he didn't scare me. I had the killer-bee instinct.

I turned the throttle and roared off around the

house, and when the diner came into sight I took aim with my paint gun and pulled the trigger. Instantly an orange splat appeared on the silver siding. "Yes," I thought. "Freddy feels very powerful." And then I went looking for Dad.

He was driving across the uneven cornfield. Light snow kicked up behind his wide tires along with loose cornstalks and chunks of frozen dirt. He looked over his shoulder and saw me coming straight at him. He turned sideways and stopped, then lifted his paint gun, aimed, and fired. The first few missed, but as I got closer he started finding his range and one hit me in the helmet with a huge thwacking sound and my head jerked back, and then a few more hit me directly in the face mask and the yellow paint burst open as if my eyeballs had just erupted.

"Awesome!" I shouted. Then one hit me in the chest and knocked the breath out of me. "That's gonna leave a mark," I added.

I turned away and ran my gloved hand over my mask to wipe the paint off so I could see, and then I circled around and headed straight for him. He headed straight for me. It was like old-fashioned jousting. I kept one hand on my throttle and with the other I raised my paint gun and fired. He did the same. Paintballs zinged back and forth. Some collided and exploded in midair. They pinged against the front fenders of the ATV and smacked me hard across my legs. I kept pulling the trigger and the orange blotches exploded across his ATV. I roared over the field toward him, and he roared toward me. Neither of us flinched. We kept firing. By the time we were ten feet apart we were blasting each other with direct hits all the way until we were at point-blank range. Then we skimmed past each other and circled around and did it again, and again, until we had to stop and reload and change power cartridges. Then we were at each other again. He was better than I was because he could steady his gun with one arm while driving with the other. I was soaked with yellow splat marks and my skin was stinging as if I were shot with arrows. After another jousting pass he slowed down and looked over his shoulder as he yelled, "You had enough?"

"No way!" I shouted back. I roared forward and circled around again. As we headed toward each other, firing wildly, his front wheel hit a rut and the ATV bounced up into the air, and when it came down he hit his seat hard and pitched off the back and onto the ground. His paint gun flew out of his hands and his ATV sputtered forward for a moment and then slowed to a stop. I was coming at him as fast as I could and he saw that I was going to be all over him before he got to his ATV. He turned to look for his paint gun and by then I was about twenty feet from him. I began to fire as quickly as I could. I braked my ATV and jumped off and ran at him firing the entire time. He tripped on the jagged cornstalks and I danced around him and fired and no matter which way he turned I had a shot at his mask and I knew he couldn't see a thing and I got closer and kept blasting him from all angles like the big man I was.

"Enough!" he cried out as he crawled forward. "I give, I give!" He held his gloved hands in front of his face but I kept giving it to him. *Splat! Splat! Splat!* I fired until the orange paintballs blended together and turned him into one big, yowling orange blob.

"I said to stop it!" he sputtered angrily.

I got him a few more times and then I just heard a hissing sound. I was out of ammo. He stood up and reached blindly for me as if his eyes had been poked out, but I was too fast for him and jumped back onto my ATV and roared across the field toward the house.

"Don't mess with Freddy," I howled. "He is one tough customer. One bad dude. One *hombre muy malo!*"

"You are dead meat!" Dad shouted. "I'm *loco* now."

I pulled up in front of the diner and grabbed my ammo bag. The front door was locked so I ran around back to the kitchen door. I went in and snatched a towel and wiped the yellow paint off my face mask, then rubbed it over my helmet and clothes. I was panting and my blood was pumping like never before. I could feel my welts throbbing but there was no time to think about pain. His ATV skidded across the gravel. In a moment I heard him yank on the front door. He pulled so hard the entire diner kind of jerked forward. Then he remembered he had the keys.

I put in a fresh power cartridge and loaded up another hundred and fifty shots. He must have done the same because the moment he unlocked the door and entered he was ready for a showdown at the Beehive Diner. I slid into a kneeling position behind the coffee counter, steadied the paint gun, and fired. He dove behind a bench seat in a booth and fired back and we just kept firing away at each other until both of us had to reload and then we did it again and by the time we were out of paintballs the diner was totally trashed. Yellow and orange paint dripped down from the ceiling and walls. The clock was hit, the stacks of plates, the coffeemakers, the griddle—everything was spattered with paint.

"Wow," I said, looking around and waving a paper napkin over my head. "Truce."

"Truce," he echoed, and the moment I set my paint gun down he made his move. In two quick steps he had me pinned on the floor.

"Just who do you think you are?" he said, crushing me with his body weight.

"I'm Freddy," I wheezed.

"So when I say 'I give up,' what are you supposed to do?"

"Take advantage of you," I replied, panting as I tried to squirm away.

"That's my boy!" he said proudly.

Just then Mom walked in through the kitchen door. I stared up at her and her mouth was hanging open. Then she looked down at us. "Do I have to separate you two already?" she asked.

"Oh, no," Dad said. "This is love."

"Then kiss and make up," she said.

We banged our helmets together because that's about as close as we could get to a kiss and he gave me a bear hug.

"You gave me a great gift today," he whispered. "That forgiveness means the world to me. It's like receiving a bucket of good karma. Tomorrow I'm playing the Christmas dates and, baby, I have a feeling you will be living in Snow White's castle."

I'd like that, I thought to myself. Even Grumpy looked happy there.

11

THE NOISE INSIDE

You can't imagine how much trouble that paintball gun caused me. I started doing bad things right away. I was hanging out in the shot-up diner like a time bomb that never stopped going off. Dad said he'd give me twenty bucks if I'd clean up all the dried paint, but I hadn't lifted a finger. The diner was still splattered with paint and looked like the inside of an insane person's mind. A few weeks ago I would have had the job done in record time, but now I just didn't care. I stretched out across the coffee counter like a sniper with my finger on the trigger.

Maybe the paintball battle with Dad had made me insane, too, because without thinking I did something really sick. I shot poor little Quesadilla. She was walking through the diner when I impulsively aimed my paint gun and shot her on the rear. She yelped and went running for the door, but it was closed so she hid under one of the booths. Her yelp snapped me out of my insane mood. I felt so bad that I got down on my hands and knees and crawled across the dirty floor to where she was cornered. "I'm sorry. I'm so, so sorry," I said. She cowered in fear when she saw me and began to quiver and I didn't know what else to say besides "I'm sorry," so I held the paint gun out and shot myself in the rear. Oh, that hurt to the core!

This didn't have anything to do with my old "wired" ways. I had my med patch on my arm. But ever since I quit school and killed Joey off, there was nothing much for me to do. Dad was always out running around searching for good karma. He came home late one night and announced that he had stood outside a nursing home all day and had walked eighty-seven old people across the street and then had walked seventy-five of them back and then had played the number one hundred and sixty-two for the Daily Number lottery. This is the kind of nutty guessing game he was doing all day now that his full-time business was trying to win the lottery. It was snowing one day and I saw him counting flakes sticking against the window where he was sitting. So far he had not hit it "big."

Mom was always out of the house because, as she said, once she had the baby she was not going to have the time to shop as much as she liked. When I asked about school she said she was counting on me to help out with Heinzie because Charles wasn't good with diapers. That left Freddy alone to do whatever he felt like doing, and that was the problem. I guess that once you give up who you are, you can become anybody, because I was far different from who I had been a few weeks ago. There just seemed to be something missing within me and I became an unthinking thing stalking the grounds and doing dumb stuff all day long.

From my bedroom window I shot at squirrels as they scampered from branch to branch. Outside I ambushed Mom in the minivan and shot the hubcaps so that they looked like the spin art you make at carnivals. I stretched out flat on my back and shot straight up into the air so they would come down and hit me. I even tried to catch them with my mouth. If a bird flew by I tried to hit it. I threw diner china up into the air and shot at it like a Wild West cowboy. I made a zigzag obstacle course of snowmen and women and children then drove around them in my ATV and shot them up until they looked like orange slush. "Freddy is very aggressive," I said slyly as I roared in circles.

I even stood in the diner bathroom and shot myself in the small mirror—right where I thought my heart might be, but it didn't hurt one bit. When I became Freddy I must have left Joey's heart behind and I didn't know if I'd ever get it back again. Even though I understood that not being myself was bad for me, I couldn't stop. I had become someone I didn't know and someone I couldn't say no to.

And then I went too far. One Sunday morning I was sitting in a living room chair with the paint gun on my lap because I had given myself a time-out. I was trying to settle down because when I was outside I really wanted to shoot at passing cars. I kept aiming at them but knew that if I pulled the trigger it would lead to police trouble, so I ran inside the house and threw myself into a chair. I started counting silently to one hundred while I breathed slowly and tried to think nice, calm thoughts when the next thing I knew I aimed the gun and shot the star off the top of the Christmas tree. In the blink of an eye there was an explosion of orange paint as the star hit the ceiling, clattered off the wall, and crashed to the floor, where it split into pieces. "Wow!" I cried. "Shooting star! Make a wish!"

Mom had not left the house yet and the look of fury on her face was pretty scary.

"Give that to me," she demanded.

"I didn't mean to do it," I whined, and hugged my paint gun. "I was just fooling around."

"I thought you were mature enough for this," she said, gripping the gun. "But clearly I was wrong."

"I'll change my ways," I said, pleading. "I won't fool around with it anymore."

"Fooling around has made a fool out of you," she

said sternly, and yanked it away from me. "You are soon going to be a big brother so you better start thinking about being a good example. But keep this up and I'll boot you off to military academy."

I began to cry. "Please, please," I begged. "Please give me another chance." I wiped my big, shiny eyes and peeked up at her. "Besides," I squeaked, "the tree has been up for a month already. It needs to come down."

"That's not the point!" she bellowed as she leaned over me. "Now, you better straighten up or you will never see this gun again. Go take a bath and think about being a little more mature." She pointed the paint gun at my feet. "Now march!" she ordered.

I stood up and marched stiffly toward the bathroom like the wooden Nutcracker. As soon as I touched the doorknob a paintball whizzed by my ear and splattered on the door. I whipped around and crouched down in fear.

"That was an accident," she cried out. "I'm so sorry. I don't know what came over me."

I knew it was an accident. That was the whole problem. Once you got that paint gun in your hands you just couldn't keep your finger off the trigger.

"It's okay," I said. "I know the feeling."

I had taken so many baths over the past weeks there was a permanent orange paint ring around the tub. The hot water helped soothe the welts on my skin. After Dad and I shot each other up on Christmas I was covered with welts the size of quarters. My chest, belly, and the front of my legs were the worst. My face was okay because of the mask and neck protector. But he did plant a good shot on my ear, which made it swell up and turn as purple as a plum.

I didn't think Dad's behavior was very mature, but that wasn't the point. Mom was right, I had to think of my own behavior because I was going to be a big brother and I had to set a good example for little Heinzie no matter what example Charles Heinz was setting for me.

When I got out of the tub I dried off and dressed and walked over to the diner. I thought I might clean it up a bit and practice some recipes or do something other than shoot paintballs. When I arrived Dad was pacing back and forth across the length of the diner floor.

"Oh God," he moaned the moment he saw me, and kicked at the confetti of losing lottery tickets. "I am sooo bored! Bored out of my *gourd*."

"We could cook together," I suggested. "I want to make a secret sauce and call it Freddy's Funky Flavor. Or we could make magic food that turns people into our zombies and they give us their wallets. Stuff like that. What do you think?"

"I hate cooking," Dad groaned. "I've decided I only like to eat. Cooking means cleaning and I don't like to clean anymore either. I just want fun, fast food, lots of money, and no hard work."

"Wow. Now that's an example of good living," I said. "How do we do that?"

"You know," he said on an upbeat note, and looked toward me. "I always think best when I'm having fun." He glanced up at the paint-smeared clock. "If we hurry we can get to Quips Pub and catch the Steelers' playoff game. What do you think of that?"

"Right on," I said. "Give me five."

He smacked my raised hand. "Go tell your mom that us boys need to chill out for a while and we'll see her tonight and not to cook dinner."

"She hasn't cooked in months," I reminded him. "Since going on maternity leave she pretty much shops all day and brings home takeout."

"Shopping is fun," he said in a dreamy way, then suddenly made an unpleasant face. "But you have to walk around and look at stuff. I just want to go sit on my butt and hire people to shop for me."

"Hey, can we bet on the game?" I asked. "Then we can make money while sitting around watching TV."

Dad looked down on me and smiled, then he poked me on the shoulder. "That is a Heinz-size idea," he said proudly. "You got any money? I'm cash-short today."

"I have about a hundred," I said, happy as a puppy.

"Well, let's go put that nest egg to work," he cried

out cheerfully. "It's just sitting around doing nothing when it could make itself useful so *we* can be sitting around doing nothing."

"I'll go get the money and tell Mom," I said, heading for the door.

"I'll be in the minivan, warming it up," he replied.

When I went into the house I thought Mom might still be mad at me. But when I told her I was going to Quips Pub she perked up. "I like it when you guys do grownup things together. Remember, you will be Heinzie's role model. So what you learn from Charles you will teach the baby. Now go out and have a great time together."

I could hear Dad beeping the horn.

"Can I bring anything back for you?" I asked.

"Sure," she chirped. "They sell those extra-extra-large Quips Pub jerseys. One of those would be nice."

"Okay," I said.

"And if they have a matching one for the baby, get that too. And when I was there a few weeks ago they had Steeler bobbleheads. If there are any left get some of those, too. We can start a collection."

"Yep," I said.

"And bring me back one of their big pretzels with the chunky salt all over it," she said, and sucked on her finger as she thought about what else she might want.

"What if I just bring you back one of everything?" I suggested.

"That'll do," she said, smiling. "Have fun."

"Oh, one more thing," I added. I reached into my pocket and pulled out the key to my ATV. "You can have this," I offered.

"For what?" she asked, puzzled.

"In case you have to get to the hospital," I explained. I pointed to her belly. "For Heinzie."

"You must be out of your mind," she replied, smiling. "Pregnant women don't drive themselves to the hospital on an ATV."

"Well, if you go pretty fast we are only like ten minutes away from the Lime Street emergency entrance at the hospital."

"I'll call a taxi," she said. "But don't worry. Now go." She waved her hand at me like chasing off a chicken. "Go," she repeated. "And have some fun with your dad."

When we arrived at Quips there were a lot of disappointed men milling around outside because the pub was already full. But Dad was one of those guys who knew that money changed sadness into happiness.

"It's reserved seating only," the doorman explained to Dad when we reached for the front door.

"Give me a twenty," Dad whispered to me, and stuck out his hand. I gave him the bill.

"I believe you have a reservation for Heinz," Dad said to the doorman as he slipped the folded bill into the man's hand.

The doorman smiled. "Right this way," he replied to Dad, who then waved to me and we were escorted into the jam-packed pub, where we inched our way through a tight crowd until we arrived at the back wall of the room where there were two empty bar stools.

"Quick, give me fifty bucks," Dad said, and stuck out his hand. "I have to place a bet before kickoff."

I passed him the money and he elbowed his way through the crowd. Once he was out of sight I began to wonder if knowing how to bet on a football game would make me a better or worse older brother for Heinzie. And then I wondered if not going to school would make me a better or worse brother. And then I thought what if I shot little Heinzie like I shot Quesadilla? What if I shot the baby on his little padded diaper as he crawled down the hall? And then I thought, *Why is Freddy so trigger-happy anyway?*

I was still thinking about it when Dad returned and sat on his stool. "I put down the fifty for them to win and beat the ten-point spread. What do you think?"

"Here's what I'm thinking!" I said, shouting loudly as the fans screamed their lungs out.

"Yeah," he said, intently peering toward the TV.

"What if you had walked into the Turkey Hill Mini

Mart that lucky day and instead of seeing Heinz ketchup you had first seen a Snickers bar or Slim Jim or something? Would you have become Mr. Snickers?"

"Yeah. Maybe. I guess," he replied, distracted by the game because every few seconds he cupped his hands around his mouth and shouted at the TV.

"But what if you ended up becoming something you didn't like?" I asked. "Like Cap'n Crunch? Would you be calling me Little Crunchie?"

"Wouldn't happen," he said firmly, and pointed toward the TV. "Look at the stadium. They don't call that Snickers Field. Or Slim Jim Stadium. No, that's a special place called Heinz Field and I'm a special guy. It's my destiny to be Charles Heinz."

"But your destiny might not be the same as my destiny. Did you ever think of that?" I asked.

"Nonsense," he said.

"But what if you ended up becoming something you didn't like?" I asked.

"Or," he said testily, "what if you ended up becoming something I didn't like. Now watch the game."

"But I'm upset with myself," I said.

"What do you mean?" he asked.

"I mean Freddy is not nice. Mom is not happy with him and she wants me to be more mature and be little Heinzie's role model, but all I do is hang around with you and do what you do."

"And what is wrong with that?" he asked. "Being like your old man is the best thing that could happen to you. Stick with me and you will be a winner."

Just then the Steelers scored and the bar crowd stood up and cheered. "Yell your lungs out!" he hollered. "Steelers rule!"

"Steelers rule!" I screamed about ten times in a row.

"See," he said hoarsely when we sat down. "Feels good to holler like a man."

That was true, because while I was screaming I wasn't thinking.

"Hey, Dad," I asked when I stopped screaming and started thinking again. "Is finding yourself different from making yourself up? Or is it the same?"

"Why are we having this discussion in the middle of a football game?" he asked.

"Because it is on my mind," I replied.

"Well, winning the lottery is on my mind," he shouted in my face. "Owning a theme park. Living in Miami. Buying a yacht. But I'm not talking about it right now."

"But it's important for me to understand who Freddy is. He confuses me and I need to figure him out before Heinzie joins us. I want to be a good older brother."

"Just go with the Freddy flow," he said, only half listening to me.

"I did," I said. "I went with the flow and that's when

I became the *evil* Freddy. Like I really loved shooting you."

"I've got news for you," he said, glancing toward the TV then back at me. "I really loved shooting you, too, and believe me, when Heinzie is old enough he'll enjoy shooting you, too."

"Can't I just stop being Freddy and be someone else?" I suggested. "Maybe someone nicer? Like I could be named Hershey after a Hershey's Kiss. Doesn't he sound nice? Or if he's too sweet I could be Tabasco Red—he sounds *spicy*."

"No," Charles replied. "You have to be Freddy. That's who you are and that is the gift you gave me and you can't take it back or trade it in for another name."

"But once you change who you are, what's to stop you from doing it all the time? I could be called A-1, like the steak sauce," I said. "Or Skittles, or Starburst, or Fritos. And you could be Mr. T or Nestea or T-Rex, it's endless. You could be somebody different every day. It's confusing."

He stood up and whistled loudly to attract a waitress carrying a tray of hot dogs and beer over her head. When she finally made it over to us he grabbed two hot dogs.

"Here," he said, handing me mine. "Shove this in your kisser and let me do the thinking." Then he grabbed a beer, too.

I gave him a worried look as I shoved the hot dog into my mouth.

"Don't worry over a little beer," he mumbled with his mouth full. "As I said, I always do my best thinking when I'm happy. Here," he offered, holding the beer toward me, "take a sip. Maybe it will make you a little happy for a change."

"No," I said. "Even if I wanted beer, it would not be the right thing to do for little Heinzie. Now, can we talk some more?"

"No!" he snapped, and threw the end of his hot dog down in frustration. "Can't we just watch the game and enjoy ourselves?"

"I need to talk," I said, kind of pleading.

"Well, I don't," he snapped back.

"But I think Freddy Heinz is a *lunatic*," I said.

He laughed. "Welcome to my world."

"But if you feel like a lunatic, too," I yelled, "why don't you just go back to who you were?"

"Because the old me is crazier than the new me," he said.

"Well, what happens when the new you gets crazier than the old you?"

"I'll cross that bridge when I get there," he said.

"Well, I'm going crazy from not knowing who I am. I mean, I don't even know what Freddy's favorite color is," I blurted out. "Did you ever think of that?"

"Stuff like that doesn't matter," he said, and turned away.

"What about his favorite TV show? Ever think of that?"

"You are buggin' me," he hollered above the crowd. "Now just relax." He twisted his back around toward me as he looked at the TV.

But as the game wore on I couldn't relax. If I was really going to be Freddy, it was necessary to discover who he was deep down inside himself because I wanted him to be as nice as Joey was. "Do you think Freddy would like pineapple on pizza?" I asked, and tapped him on the shoulder. "Joey did."

He turned back toward me. "Look," he said sternly, "before I just flip out and become Mr. Taco Bell and head for the border, here is what I need you to do. Go to the bathroom and straighten your head around and flush Joey down the toilet once and for all and when you come out you will be Freddy the very happy boy with a great future. ¿Comprendes, amigo?" he said with his jaw clenched.

"Okay," I said, feeling a little scared of him. "I'll go get my happy Freddy head on straight."

"Exactly," Dad agreed. "Now pull yourself together and remember, when in doubt just do what I do. Stop thinkin' and let your walkin' do your talkin'."

I walked down to the bathroom. It was empty because the game was still being played. I stared into the bathroom mirror then took a comb from my back pocket. "Maybe Freddy needs a new hairstyle," I said to myself. I did a part on the left, then mussed it up and did a part on the right. I didn't like that either. Then I parted it in the middle and combed half to the front down over my forehead and half toward the back. It looked totally goofy and I bobbled my head up and down and back and forth like those mindless, springy-headed dolls Mom wanted from the gift shop. I bobbled my head some more. "Hi," I said, in a robotic voice, "I am Freddy Heinz, the happy little bobblehead. I come in fifty-seven varieties. Nutty, freaky, goofy, dizzy, batty, wacky, crabby, flippy, silly, happy." Just then the crowd gasped and moaned so I yelled out, "Do you want fries with that?"

"Ohhh, no!" the crowd groaned.

"Ohhh, yes!" I replied, and bobbled my head and did a slow little bobblehead shuffle over to the toilet and gave Joey a flush and then I shuffled out of the bathroom. "Freddy is lettin' his walkin' do his talkin'," I said.

I was feeling very good about being Freddy-the-brainless-bobblehead until I ran into trouble. I was looking over the souvenirs and counting my money to see how much I had left when the woman next to me who was wearing all black and gold tapped me on my shoulder. I looked up at her and my head began to bobble out of control. It was Mrs. Ginger.

"Do I know you?" she asked, and stooped down to get a closer look at me. I was going to run but then she locked eyes with me, which just stopped me in my tracks and sucked the words right out of my chattering mouth.

"Yes," I replied. "I'm Freddy Heinz."

"That's right—Freddy. We were expecting you and then you never showed up."

"My parents decided to homeschool me," I said. "I'm going to help them run the Beehive Diner."

"Really?" She stared hard at me and I felt naked. I always felt that way when I was telling a lie. "Well, they need to register your status with the district and they need to be certified by the state. Do you know if they've done that?"

"How would I know what they do?" I said.

"You're right," she said. "It's not up to you to register yourself. I'll follow up on this, and in the meantime can you have your parents call me?"

I began to pull away from her. "Do you want fries with that?" I shouted, then turned and shuffled away.

"Have them call me!" she ordered.

"Yes," I bleated, and waved one hand overhead as I baby-stepped my way through the packed crowd. I was so nervous my head began to throb and swell, which made me worry that it would explode into a million pieces and if that happened I might have to become a million selves—only each one of me would have a tiny speck of a brain the size of plankton.

Finally I popped out of the crowd and spotted Dad. He looked grumpy. Still, it was good to see him because it got me away from my thoughts.

"What's wrong?" I asked. "I thought you had a happy beer?"

"There's just not enough action," he groaned, throwing his arms up into the air when I sat down. "Now we're losing and they're just playing patty-cake with each other."

"Too bad," I replied. "They should have paint guns and play at the same time."

"That would put some pizzazz in it," he agreed. "I should call the commissioner. We could start a Paintball Football League. Can you imagine the announcer saying, 'He's going deep—here's the pass—he reaches for it—*SPLAT!*—oh, too bad he was blindsided by a shot to the eyes.' "

"Oh, here's one more thing on my mind that I found while my walkin' was doin' my talkin'," I said.

He gave me an intensely disapproving look. "I thought you took care of that *thinking* problem," he said harshly.

"It's the last thing," I cried. "I promise. And then I'll shut up."

"What is it?"

"I just ran into the school principal," I blurted out, "and she said she was going to call the school department on me, so I think it would be good for me to go back to school and be a good example for Heinzie because I'm not doing anything around the diner besides shooting everything that moves."

Suddenly his face lit up. "Wait a minute!" he shouted, and grabbed my shoulders. "You are a genius. You can't go back to school, because something you said gave me an insanely brilliant idea, and like the smart, rich people we are going to make a *fortune* by putting our best qualities to work." His gaze seemed to drift away, out the window and toward a distant vision of our golden success. When he turned back toward me his face had that glow from when he had a big new idea—a sure winner—and I leaned toward him because I wanted that glow to light me up too and then I'd have the glow and light up little Heinzie.

"Well," I said, and pinched him. "Are you going to tell me about it?"

"Mercy!" he cried, snapping out of it. "Come on! Football is totally boring compared to what I have in mind. Besides, we lost the bet." He jumped up and began to push people out of the way. "I'll explain it on the way home," he said over his shoulder. "You'll love it."

12

BUSSED

It was a *great* idea. It was better than the name change idea. Or buying the diner and turning it into the Beehive idea. And it was far better even than trying to win the lottery all the time because it was taking the bull by the horns and working for success instead of waiting for chance to do all the heavy lifting for us.

Here is how he explained the idea on the drive home from Quips. "First," he declared, pumping his fist with pride, "it is a plan to make money sticking to the Charles Heinz standards of labor management. It is not boring. It is fast. It is breezy-easy. It will keep you busy. It will make us rich. And once we get it up and going, we can hire people to run the diner so we don't have to cook and clean, and then we can chill out and roll in the dough as we build our empire."

"Well, don't keep me waiting," I begged. "What is it?"

"Picture this," he said, glancing between me and the road.

"It's human nature to want to shoot something—right?" he asked.

"Right," I confirmed. "Mom even took a shot at me today."

"That proves my point," he concluded. "We'll simply take advantage of what people like to do—which is to shoot each other."

"I like to do it, but I don't think it's a good thing," I said doubtfully.

"This isn't about right or wrong—this is about business. I propose we build a kind of outdoor shooting range. We have a raised platform at one end of a fenced-in area about the size of a tennis court. On the platform we have a dozen mounted superpowerful paintball guns. And now here is the *genius* part. We put you back in that big padded bee costume and give you some more padding and protective head gear and you buzz around the fenced-in area like a big menacing bee and people pay to shoot at you."

"What do you do?" I asked.

"I collect the money. We'll charge like a buck for five shots, three bucks for twenty shots and so on. I'll hand out the paintballs and service the guns," he said.

"Can I add to your idea?" I asked.

"Sure," he said. "Shoot."

"Well, can we decorate the field with bee stuff. Like a beehive. And some wooden flowers and a big jar of honey—stuff like that, so it would look more fun and give me a chance to hide."

"Well, okay, but you can't hide too much," he cautioned. "People are going to want to have a clean shot at you. I think mostly you need to run around."

"How about the dogs?" I asked.

"Wow! Good idea," he said, getting even more excited. "There must be combat padding for military dogs. Your mom will know where to buy it."

"And can I ride my ATV?" I asked.

"Maybe," he said, considering it. "We can paint it black and yellow to match the minivan."

"That would be cool," I said.

"Oh," he cried with excitement. "And one more thing. You'll have to have a bullhorn and yell a steady stream of insults at the shooters. You know, egg 'em on so they get really mad at you and fire a lot of shots because the faster they shoot the more money we make."

"Can I say *anything*?" I asked.

"Within reason," he replied. "You have to figure this is going to be a family audience, so no curse words."

"Yeah," I said, bobbing my head up and down. "Saying anything I want is like a dream come true for Freddy."

"I was thinking we'd call it Shoot the Busy Bee."

"Or Sting the Busy Bee," I suggested, "because that's what bees do."

"Yeah," he said, uncertain. "Though I sure like the word *shoot* in there. People are attracted to that word like bees to honey."

"Well, you can put up a billboard on the side of the road telling people they can shoot paintballs at the Busy Bee," I said.

"Yeah," he said. "Then over time we can expand the concept. You can dress up as a deer and we'll have paintball deer-hunting season. We can call that one Shoot-to-Kill. Or your mom can dress up like a crazy shopper chasing after bargains, or I can find Dick the thief and we can have Shoot-the-Criminal-Escapee and he can wear a black-and-white-striped suit. Once we get going we can have a row of themes."

"Don't forget Shoot-Your-Lousy-Kid!" I shouted.

"Excellent!" he yelled back. We high-fived. "I can see this idea right before my eyes, just like the first time I saw those winning lottery numbers."

It was like having him in charge allowed me to just go with the flow. As he talked I said, "Yeah," and "yeah," like the Freddy bobblehead I was, until we couldn't think of anything else to add to the big, beautiful idea that was the beginning of my Freddy future, an incredible future which was bright and hopeful and made me think that being Freddy was going to work out just like Mom promised. I'd have the Sting the Busy Bee business and diner and Dad and I would make money and we'd be able to raise little Heinzie to follow in our successful footsteps, and Mom would have enough money to shop and be happy and if she wanted we could buy her a nail salon and put it next to the diner and we could call it Ten Little Fingers or The Hand of Heinz and she could hire people to work for her, too.

Then he said, "One more thing. We'll have to wait till the spring to build it 'cause the ground has to thaw."

"Dang," I said, disappointed, and punched myself in the thigh. But then I pulled myself together. "Well, that will give me time to practice my insults."

"That's thinking positive," he said, and rapped his knuckles on my helmet, which I still liked to wear in the car. "Now you'll have plenty of time to cook up some really rude things."

But Dad was as impatient as I was. Even though we were not going to build it until spring, he got off to a fast start. He drew out elaborate plans for the paintball shooting gallery. He ordered fencing and lumber and bags of cement. But when the truck arrived, Dad got into a shouting match with the driver, who wanted cash on delivery and wouldn't take a credit card.

When the truck left with our stuff, I asked Dad if he was mad.

"Not really," he said. "By the time the ground thaws I'll have figured out how to crack the lottery bank and we'll have enough cash to *hire* a company to build the paintball court. I don't know what I was thinking by ordering the supplies."

"Yeah," I said. "Maybe we dodged a bullet."

"You got that right," he said, and poked my shoulder. "We just want to make the money. Let someone else do the heavy lifting."

"Yeah," I said. "That's the Heinz way of thinking."

While we waited for warmer weather Charles went back to making lists of numbers so he could win more money and plan for our paintball theme park empire. I rolled up my sleeves and got to work because when my hands are busy I'm not thinking of weird things to do. I cut up cardboard boxes into large flowers and bees and other bugs. I even cut out little doghouses and fire hydrants for El Gordo and Quesadilla to hide behind. Then I painted them and propped them up against the booths to dry.

But not everyone was waiting for our empire to grow. On one of those sunny winter days, Dad and I were working up a practice session for the paintball game. I was in the bee costume with my bullhorn and he stood about a hundred feet away from me and tried to hit me. I was yelling out insults and running in figure eights and his shots were missing me pretty good, but a few hit me. "What are you? Some kind of a girlie man!" I hollered, ducking down behind one of my large tulips. "Hit me in the bee-hind!" I yelled, and stuck my rear out to the side to give him a target.

Just when Dad planted a direct hit on my stinger and I flopped to the ground, a car pulled up and a stranger stepped out. He was in a dark suit and carried a briefcase. Dad lowered his paint gun and looked at him suspiciously. I came running in to see what was going on.

I arrived when the man said, "My name is Mr. Paxson and I'm with the Lancaster school board."

"So?" Dad said, and squinted at him.

"You might call me a truant officer," he explained further. "I'm here to check up on a boy named Freddy Heinz. Some time ago we received a notification from the principal at Keystone that a kid was living here who wasn't going to school. And recently she called to follow up. Said she saw him and he still wasn't in school."

After he said that last bit he looked down at me. I had some paint dripping down the side of my helmet and onto my costume. "Buzzzzz," I said.

"While you've been meaning to check up on him," Dad said, "we've made other educational arrangements."

"You'll have to excuse me," Mr. Paxson replied. "I have a huge caseload and I've been slow to get out here. You would be surprised to know how many kids don't go to school."

"So you mean a kid could fall between the cracks before you find him?" Dad asked, and from the tone of his voice I knew he was hoping that I had done just that—fallen between the cracks.

"Or he could just be *hiding* between the cracks," Mr. Paxson suggested as he pointed at me. "Maybe like this kid."

Dad looked at me then back at Mr. Paxson. "He's being homeschooled," he explained.

"And what are you teaching him?" Mr. Paxson asked, nodding toward the paint gun.

"This is part of the physical education program," Dad replied in his official voice. "At regular school they have dodgeball. Well, we don't have a lot of kids so we play dodge the paintball."

"Are you aware that this could look like *abuse* to me?" Mr. Paxson stated firmly.

"Freddy," Dad said with mock concern in his voice, "am I abusing you?"

I lifted the bullhorn to my lips and pointed it at Mr. Paxson. *"No!"* I shouted. *"I live for this game!"*

Mr. Paxson stepped back a pace. "I see," he said while wiggling a pinky finger in his ear hole. "Well, what about"—he paused and looked at his notes—

"Joey Pigza? The principal wanted me to ask about him. Is he around?"

"*He disappeared!*" I shouted through the bullhorn before Charles could say anything.

"Do you know where he went?" Mr. Paxson asked as he motioned for me to lower the bullhorn.

"You won't find him ever again," I replied.

"Why not?" he pressed.

" 'Cause trying to find him is like trying to find a breath of air you had last year—it's impossible."

"Then what about you?" he asked. "Tell me about this homeschooling."

"I'm in a special program where I'm learning how to be a chef at the diner," I said, and kicked a clod of dirt toward it.

"What program is that?"

"Mail order," Charles said abruptly. "And I think you've asked enough questions."

"For now I have," Mr. Paxson replied without flinching. "But I'll be back for more answers. The state requires certification for homeschool situations, so you better get your papers in order." Then he turned and walked toward his car. When he opened the door I hollered through the bullhorn, "*Kiss my honey-dipped doughnuts!*"

Dad yanked the bullhorn out of my hand. "What are you doing?" he snapped, his eyes bugging out in anger. "That guy could be trouble."

"I'm just practicing my insults," I said. "Like you told me."

"Well, now I'm telling you to get in the house. I don't want that guy breathing down my neck and looking for Joey Pigza."

The next morning Dad had me clean up around the grill so I could work on my cooking homework and pretend I was being homeschooled in case the truant officer returned. I made pancakes and eggs and sausage and toast. Mom came in from the house and I loaded up her plate.

"This is the best food I've ever eaten," she said, wolfing it down.

"Would you give me an A for cooking today?" I asked.

"Definitely," she said. "It's given me a burst of energy."

"What are you doing with your energy?"

"Some final shopping!" she said. "There's just a million things a woman needs when she is going to have a baby."

"By the way," she said, turning toward Dad as she dug a credit card out of her pocket. "I was doing some online shopping just now and my credit card was refused." She threw it on the table.

"I bet," he said, half distracted by his list of numbers. "That's happened to me before and it's a total bummer."

"A huge bummer," she said testily. "I called the credit card company and they said I was 'maxed out' and late with a payment."

"Tell them that's a temporary problem," Dad replied.

"*You* tell them," she said, "because it's too stressful for me to deal with. I swear when he said 'maxed out' I almost had little Heinzie on the spot."

"Don't work yourself into a panic," Charles said. "It's just a little mix-up with the credit bureau." Then he started making a list of numbers again.

After a moment she said, "Well, aren't you going to do something? You know today's the day my girl-friends are taking me for a three-day spa treatment for a baby shower, and I'll need some credit."

"Sure," he replied. "Now come here so I can rub your belly for good luck. I won a few bucks the last time I did it."

"I guess so," Mom groaned. "But make it snappy. I'm itchin' to hit the road."

He rubbed her belly and then he put his lips against her skin and whispered, "Little Heinzie. If you hear me, knock three times." He pulled his head back and placed his palm on her belly. Suddenly his face lit up and he turned to us. "He just kicked me three times," he said joyfully. "I felt it."

Then he placed his lips against her skin again. "Give me the first number," he whispered. He waited.

We waited, and waited. But nothing happened. Finally Mom couldn't wait any longer.

"I've got to get going," she said, backing away and pulling her shirt down. "My belly isn't a Ouija board."

"But babies can see into the future," Charles said.

"Well, I hope it looks better than what I see," she said scornfully. "Now give me your credit card, I can't wait for you to conjure up a winner." She stuck out her hand.

Dad pulled out his wallet and gave her one that had both their names on it.

"Thanks, sugar," she said, taking the card and kissing him on the head. Then she turned toward me. "Freddy, go in the house and put those two bags of baby shower gifts in the car for me."

"I thought your friends gave you gifts at the shower?" Charles said.

"Honey," she replied, "it makes me feel good to buy things for my friends, which is why I have friends and you two just have each other and the *perros*. Now you want me to be your dream angel, don't you, sweetie?"

"Of course, sugar," he replied. "You go wear that credit card out and we'll see you in a few days."

I took the bags of gifts to the car and said goodbye to her, and when I returned to the diner Dad was sitting there with his head in his hands.

"Freddy," he called when he looked up.

"Yeah, Dad?" I answered.

"Get me that stack of mail out of my post office."

I trotted down to the end of the diner, where Dad had taken over a second booth and called it his "post office." There was a stack of credit card letters.

"Do you want these bills?" I hollered back.

"They're not bills," he said. "Just bring them to me."

I carried them back to him and he opened the top envelope and pulled out a card. "Here's your first credit card," he said, holding it up. I read the name on it—JOEY PIGZA. "Now sign it on the back."

"Don't you have to be an adult?" I asked.

"You're not in school," he replied. "That means you are an adult."

"But the name says Joey," I pointed out.

"Exactly," he replied, and winked at me. "So billing him will be like trying to bill a breath of air you had last year."

"Is this criminal?" I asked.

"We're just making our own luck," he explained. "Now sign, and when we build our paintball empire we'll pay it all back."

"But what if I can't pay it?"

"Don't worry, they won't throw a kid in jail for debt."

I really didn't know what to say but for just a moment, a quick little moment, I knew that something smelled rotten. It was one of those moments that if you were with the wrong kind of people you would take off running for your life. But since I was with Dad

I just did as I was told. I signed the back of the card.

"Great!" he said.

I didn't know what to say so I said, "Do you want fries with that card?"

"Maybe later," he said, "but right now I feel something different coming over me."

"Like what? A cold?" I asked.

"No. Just something like a seed sprouting out of the ground. You know, like something inside me wants to break out and come to life."

"Maybe you feel spring coming on," I suggested.

"I can't wait for that," he said with sudden determination as he stood up. "I'm going to do it now. I'm going to take the plunge and do it!" He pounded his fist on the table.

"What do you mean?" I asked.

"The face change," he said, unfolding a brochure. "The plastic surgery I told you about."

I sat down next to him and looked. You could pick from a list of noses, eye treatments, chin implants, cheek implants, eyebrow shapes, lip sizes—it was like playing Mr. Potato Head with all the mix-and-match features. He had already circled a few changes he wanted to make.

"Aren't you afraid of getting all cut up?" I asked.

"Nah," he said bravely. "That part doesn't scare me. But I do have this one oddball fear that after the bandages come off I'm going to look into the mirror and not know who the heck I am. You know what I mean?"

"I do," I replied. "Because once I gave up being Joey it took me a while to figure out who Freddy was."

"Exactly," he agreed. "I worry that might happen to me, too, and I'll have to go make myself up all over again."

"Then don't chance it," I said. "Besides, can't you just wait until Heinzie is born?"

"I want to have my face changed now so I don't confuse the baby," he said. "I want little Heinzie to bond with the new Charles. I don't want him seeing my old Carter face. He'd think he had two dads!"

"Well, how are you going to pay for it?" I asked now that I knew we were running out of money.

He grinned and held up the new credit card with my old name on it. "Now that you've given me a little rainy day cash," he said, slipping the card into his pocket, "I'm all set. Besides, if I don't spend this on my face now, I may never get another chance. With the way your mom runs through cash," he said, waving his arms overhead, "this whole place will be out of operation."

In a few minutes he called the private clinic. They just had a cancellation and could take him immediately. "See," he said after he hung up the phone. "Nothing to worry about. Luck is on my side."

"But you can't leave me by myself. I'm just a kid."

"Don't kid yourself, Freddy. Be a man. You're old

enough to handle a couple days on your own. Besides, you know where to reach me if you need me."

Within an hour the dogs and I followed him outside with his tote bag of clothes where a taxi was waiting. "I should be home before your mom, but if not she'll be home in a few days," he said. "But whatever you do," he warned me, "don't answer the door, and don't answer the phone, and it would be best if you don't play outside."

"What can I do then?" I asked.

"I think you need to come up with some special Freddy Fries," he suggested. "Something hot and spicy we can sell at the paintball gallery."

"Okay, I'll work on it," I said, and turned to go.

"One more thing," he called out, grinning at me. "Take a last look at this beat-up old face because you are going to be blinded by a superstar face the next time you lay eyes on me."

I took a good look at him, and thought to myself it didn't matter if I remembered his old face or not. I'd just have to adjust to whatever changes he made.

Once the cab pulled out onto the road, I went back into the house. I climbed up to my room. There was a lot to think about with so much happening, and happening quickly. Soon Mom was going to have a baby. Charles was going to have a baby face and I needed to baby myself. I took off my old patch and tossed it in the trash, then put a fresh one on.

"Get ready, Freddy," I said to myself. "I smell trouble."

I stood up to look out my window because it was better than looking into my own panicky mind. I stared at the tree. It was still dark brown, but where the new branches and leaves would arrive were small green nubs already poking up like noses to sniff the air and make sure that it was safe to come out all the way. The new leaves didn't take chances. Even though winter had been light those leaves were waiting for the sun to warm them up and only then would they peek out like kitten eyes opening for the first time. Then they'd grow larger and stronger until once again they'd look like those leaf hands waving for me in the warm wind, and no matter what trouble came my way we'd hang on together.

13

WHAT GOES AROUND

As Mom's doctor said, we needed a family apartment at the hospital once all four of us suddenly found ourselves living there.

I was the first one to check in.

Mom and Dad had left the house the day before. I'd spent most of my time watching TV and playing with the dogs until I got bored. Then I locked myself up in the diner kitchen and started cooking up some gourmet Freddy Fries. It was actually great to be alone because I could finally get some cooking done without Dad telling me not to make a mess, or Mom telling me what food smells made her tummy "churn." I had already invented Salsa-Seasoned Fries for the Paintball Empire and I was working on K-9 Freddy Fries. I pounded up a bunch of dog biscuits with a hammer then rolled the cut-up potatoes in the crumbs and let them sit for a minute. Then I dressed the dogs for dinner with little white napkins tied around their necks and I sat them on the counter stools. I had given them each a little doggy menu I made with only one choice—K-9 Freddy Fries. I had taken their food order and given them their own bowls of water, then stepped back into the kitchen to lower the basket of K-9 Fries in the boiling Frialator oil. Suddenly there was pounding on the front door. It startled me and the dogs began to bark and they jumped down from their stools. I went into the front of the diner. It was already dark but I could make out a big man banging his forehead on the glass.

"What do you want?" I hollered.

"It's Dick!" he wailed. "Carter's old friend Dick."

I hadn't seen him since the wedding, when he got drunk and Dad had to ask him to leave the reception. Dad had fed him at Thanksgiving but now he was back. I thought maybe he was hungry again.

"Please, let me in," he cried. He waved a fistful of money over his head then pounded on the door again.

I thought he was going to break the glass so I said, "Okay, just a minute." I figured some Freddy Fries would settle him down and then he'd leave. He could be my first human diner customer.

But as soon as I unlocked the door he lunged at me like a drunken polar bear. "Here's your money!" he roared, and tried to wrap his arms around me. The tears streamed from his eyes and his drunken breath was awful. He held up the money for me to see then lunged at me again. I didn't have my helmet on and as I stepped back I tripped over El Gordo, who yelped as I flew backward, and slammed my head against the sharp edge of the coffee counter. All I could picture in my brain was the sound of a baseball bat snapping. My head bounced up and as I dropped toward the floor I smacked my head on the metal footrest that jutted up from the bottom of the stool. I didn't black out but I almost wished I had because Dick just leaned over me and he was wringing his hands and blubbering and asking what he should do next.

"Call 911," I whispered. "I think I recracked my head." It was throbbing.

He called them and then he stood over me. "I'm so sorry," he said. "You're bleeding."

"Is it red liquid, or white?" I asked.

"Red," he said, pressing on it with napkins.

"That's better," I guessed. "I just don't want my brain leaking out."

"I'm sorry," he said again. "I was just trying to return the money. I have all five grand of it."

"It's fine," I said. "Just turn off the fryer and take care of the dogs. You can stay at the house."

Dick nodded.

Then I closed my eyes and Dick held my hand and we waited quietly for the ambulance to arrive, and when it did they carefully picked me up and put me on a special neck-and-head-brace stretcher and we raced toward the hospital.

"Am I going to be okay?" I asked the EMT who was taking my temperature.

"You look familiar," he replied. "Aren't you the same kid who did this last year?"

"I don't know," I said. "Last time I was knocked out."

"What's your name?"

"That's kind of a confusing question," I said.

"You better rest," he suggested after giving me a careful look. "I think it's just a bad cut. Everything will be fine."

And it was.

In the ER, they wanted to know how to find my parents. I told them Mom was at a spa and Dad was at the downtown face clinic.

"Oh, the *butcher* shop" is what one doctor remarked. He seemed to know the clinic I was talking about. Then they stitched me up.

I fell asleep on my little curtained-off bed. When I woke up I couldn't turn my head at all because I had a plastic brace on my neck and my head was still wrapped up as if they were trying to keep it from splitting open like a broken egg. But I looked worse than I felt.

When the nurse saw I was awake she came over to my bed and gave me a sip of water.

"Don't worry about your head," she said. "It's fine. The doctor just put the brace on your neck to keep you from rolling around in your sleep."

"Thanks," I said as she removed it.

"And here's something else I don't want you to worry about," she said. "Your mother is here."

"To visit me?"

"Not just yet," she replied. "At the moment she is a patient on the maternity ward. She just had a baby."

"But it's not due yet," I said.

"No one told the baby that," she said.

"Can I visit her?" I asked the nurse.

She glanced at her watch. "Sure," she said. "There's a spare bed in her room, so you can stay with her."

The nurse helped me stand up and I walked like a robot onto an elevator and we went up a floor and off to Mom's room, where she was resting.

The nurse sat me in Mom's wheelchair then left us alone. Mom was dozing and I stared at her until she opened her eyes and blinked as if she had just come out of a dream and didn't know where she was. She had a tube in her arm and looked as if she were a deflated balloon they were trying to blow back up.

"It's me, Freddy," I said.

"Oh, sweetie, I heard you were here," she said with

concern, and she raised her arms for me to come hug her.

"I heard about you, too," I said, and wheeled my way over to the side of her bed.

"What happened?" she asked. "And where's your father?"

"You tell me your story first," I said as I leaned over and hugged her. "My busted head story is about the same dumb thing as before, only this time not so bad."

She smiled. "My birth story is about the same as when I had you, too. But not so bad, either. I'm just really sore."

"Does that mean Heinzie is a boy like me?"

"Yes," she said. "Another nutty boy who showed up early just like you did. The two of you have no patience."

"Can I see him?"

"In a little bit," she said. "He's in the intensive care unit, but they promised to bring me to him for some special mother love when he's ready."

"Why'd he come early?"

"I was a little more pregnant than what they thought and I did something stupid. I was at the spa with the girls and this morning we all had facials and massages and then they talked me into going into the hot tub, which was a mistake. I overheated and suddenly I had a terrible pain in my belly that wouldn't go away and I got lobster red and my blood pressure shot up and the girls hauled me out of the tub and into the minivan and drove me to the emergency room, where the baby was in a 'fragile' state and I had to have an emergency cesarean section. The baby is fine. He was just a little early, is all."

And then I heard Dad's voice say, "And I'm a bit late."

He was the last of the Heinz family to arrive. I looked toward the door but wouldn't have known it was him unless he told me because he had white gauze bandages wrapped in circles from his neck up to the top of his head where just a few dark hairs stuck out like oily weeds. All I could see of his face were two beady eyes and a greasy brown food stain on the gauze around his swollen lips.

"What happened to you?" I asked as he staggered through the doorway and moaned like a mummy in a scary old movie.

"Complications," he whispered painfully. "Infection set in."

That gave me the willies.

Mom had a different reaction. "I can't believe you left Freddy alone and then missed the birth of your own son—again!" she said. She slapped the bed so hard she jerked the tube and I had to hop up to catch the metal stand before it fell over.

"Relax," Dad said, but that only made it worse.

"And then you went and got your face rearranged without telling me," she continued, still angry. "You know I wanted mine done, too."

"I wanted it to be a surprise," he mumbled.

"Oh," she said, wincing as she sat up a bit. "And here's another surprise."

"Mom," I said quietly, "you should stay calm."

It must have hurt Charles to talk because he just nodded in agreement with what I said.

"How can I be calm when the credit card he gave me was refused by the hospital?" she said crossly. "And this is going to cost a fortune," she continued, pointing toward us all.

"Guess I won the lottery of bad luck," Dad said softly, as he slowly shook his head back and forth.

"Well, what goes around comes around," Mom said, sounding tired again.

"But I have good news," I said, suddenly remembering. "Dick returned with the money he owed Dad."

"What?" Dad said, perking up when I mentioned money.

"That's how I cut my head," I explained. "He came by with the money and scared me and I fell down."

"Do you know where he is?" Dad asked.

"At the diner," I replied. "He's taking care of the dogs. Or they're taking care of him."

Dad let out a painful snuffle. "Don't make me laugh," he begged. "It pulls on my stitches."

He stood up. The way he was bandaged made him look like his brain had been amputated. "Freddy," he said, "let's allow your mom to rest."

"See you later," I said, and blew her a kiss. She blew one back.

We were not out of the room for two seconds when Dad said to me in his reedy voice, "Did you see the cash in Dick's hand?"

"Yeah," I replied. "It was about the last thing I did see."

"Good," he said, straining. "Call him and have him bring the cash. But not a word to your mom."

"Sure," I said.

"I'm going to ask about the baby, then work the ER for some free advice about my face," he mumbled, and drifted off.

I went to the nurses' station and used their phone. I called Dick and gave him Dad's instructions. One of Mom's friends had left the minivan at the diner, and Dick said he would drive in with the cash and the dogs. When I got off the phone I was tired again. I went back to Mom's room. She was asleep. I curled up under the covers on the spare bed and fell asleep myself.

I don't know how long I was out but the moment I opened my eyes a nurse came in and told me if I hurried I could see the baby. Heinzie was strong enough and they had already put Mom in her wheelchair and allowed her to visit him in the intensive care unit. I followed the nurse down the hall, up the elevator, and into the viewing area, where all the premature babies were kept. There was a solid glass wall and Mom was on one side and I was directly on the other. Heinzie was in a clear plastic crib, all wrapped up in a blanket except for his tiny red face, which was lost in sleep. Mom was sitting in the wheelchair. She reached over the side of the crib and stroked the blue knit cap on his head.

"Can I go in there?" I asked the nurse.

"Not yet," she said. "We just allow mothers. We want them to touch the babies and talk to them or sing and just be sweet to them."

I stared at the side of little Heinzie's soft face. He was so cute. But because he was a boy I whispered, "He's handsome."

"He looks just like you," the nurse said to me as Mom gently stroked his blanket with the tips of her fingers.

"He's my delayed twin," I said.

Just then Dad walked up next to me. He said he had already seen Mom and the baby but he had gone down to the gift shop to buy a camera. Now he was pressing against the glass and taking pictures.

"Not with the flash on," the nurse said firmly. "We just want him to relax and bond with his mother and listen to her voice and get some love. It's the best thing for him."

"Sorry," Dad muttered as she bustled off.

"The nurse said he looks just like me as a baby," I said to him. I was so proud of that.

"I wouldn't know," Dad said, still sounding hoarse. "I missed your grand entrance into this world."

"What were you doing?" I asked. It seemed incredible that someone would miss a moment like this.

"I was throwing you a monthlong party down at the pub," he said. "I was celebrating the birth of my firstborn son. She had the agony, so I had the ecstasy. Cheers to that!"

He raised an imaginary glass and I knew if I could see his face under the bandages he'd have that twinkling leprechaun look that said, "I'm just a lovable imp who will never change."

After a while a nurse joined Mom. She wheeled little Heinzie deeper into the intensive care ward where another nurse began to arrange his crib. Then the first nurse returned to wheel Mom away.

"See you later, alligator," I mouthed.

"Bye, sweetie," Mom mouthed back.

"I'll be back in little bit," Dad said to me. "Dick should be downstairs by now and I have to go pick up a prescription."

"What about your bandages?" I asked.

"I can take them off soon," he replied.

"Can I help?" I really was curious to see what he looked like.

"Not now," he said. "Later. I want it to be a surprise."

He turned away from me and leaned forward, placing his lips against the glass. He whispered something and the words buzzed like a bee trapped against a windowpane, then he pulled away from the glass and looked down at his feet. In that moment I thought I could see two damp spots on the gauze just under his eyes.

"What's wrong, Dad?" I asked, because I suddenly felt so sad.

He didn't answer. He walked down the hallway and out the door without looking back.

I watched him go and it was as if a part of me went with him. Maybe the Freddy part. I wasn't sure.

"Wait!" I cried, and began to follow him. When I reached the door and walked out he was gone. I walked faster but I never caught up to him. I went up and down the halls but he had vanished.

When I finally returned to Mom's floor a nice older woman volunteer was knocking on her closed door.

"Can I help you?" I asked. "I'm her kid."

"I have a basket of flowers for the new mom," she said with a smile.

"I'll take them," I said.

"There's a card, too," she pointed out as I reached for the basket handle.

"Thank you."

"You are welcome, young man," she said. "Have a good day."

I opened the room door. Mom was back in bed. "Who knocked?" she asked as I entered.

"Flowers for you," I announced, and held up the basket so she could see them. Then I brought her the big card which had FRAN written on it.

The moment she saw her real name she quickly ripped open the envelope. A stack of money fell out onto her blanket, and right away I figured it was the money Dick had given back to Dad. And then Mom read the card. "The loser!" she groaned, and dropped her head back into the pillow. "I knew it! I knew he was slipping off the deep end again. I could just *kill* him!"

"What does it say?" I asked.

"He has to go find himself," she said sarcastically. "He doesn't know who he is anymore."

I wasn't surprised because I knew exactly what he meant.

"Go downstairs," she ordered angrily. "And drag his mummy-wrapped face up here. After I work *my* surgery on him he definitely won't have a clue who he is."

I wanted to say that she should just let him go but I could tell that she wasn't in the forgiving mood just yet.

I stood up as quietly as I could and went down to the lobby. The guard desk was unoccupied, so there was nobody at the door to stop me from going outside.

Dad wasn't there. I shuffled out to the parking lot and looked for the minivan. I didn't see it either. But suddenly I heard dogs barking.

"El Gordo!" I shouted. "Quesadilla!" I shuffled down a few rows of cars and spotted them hiding under the bumper of a stranger's truck in the parking lot.

"Where did you come from?" I asked as they barked and jumped back and forth and up and down. I untied their leashes from the bumper and squatted down and scratched their heads. For a moment I thought maybe Dad and Dick were still around, but when I stood up and steadied myself against the truck I saw the yellow minivan over in the corner. It was hoisted up onto the back of a tow truck like a giant busted bee.

The dogs and I walked over to where the tow truck driver was securing the minivan with heavy chains.

"Did our van break down?" I asked.

"Nope," he said. "It's being repossessed for nonpayment."

I knew what that meant. "Well, did you see some guys out here?" I asked. "One of them had his whole head wrapped up."

"Oh yeah," he said, "he was over by the front door talking with a big blond guy who had them dogs. I spotted the big guy on the road and followed him here because the dealership sent me out to get the van. The other guy was removing some bandages from his head."

"What happened next?" I asked.

He turned and pointed toward the hospital exit sign. "Once they noticed I was hooking the van up they hustled out of the parking lot and took off down Lime Street."

"Thanks," I said. I walked the dogs over to the parking lot exit sign. On the ground was a long, wide ribbon of gauze. It looked like a huge rattlesnake had shed its skin and slithered off. I looked up the street, then down, but I didn't spot them. I knew they weren't coming back. I stood there feeling beat up. It was all over. His return, the rewedding, the name change, the diner—everything went down the street with him. He had left me behind, and I was returning to my old self. And you know me—I can't stay mad for very long.

"Granny was right," I said. "When you forgive someone it does make you stronger. It makes your heart bigger than your hate."

I cupped my hands around my mouth and took a deep breath. "You don't have to run away. You can come back. I already forgave you!"

My words went down the street like a bloodhound but they didn't sniff him out.

After a minute, I yelled, "Doesn't my forgiveness mean anything to you?" I waited another minute. I wanted to holler, "Only a coward is afraid of forgiveness," but I couldn't. Instead I shouted, "Call us! You can change your face but not your family." Then I turned with the dogs and tugged them forward as we walked back to the tow truck driver.

"Any chance you can tell me what the man with the bandages looked like after he took them off?" I asked.

"Not really," he said. "Kinda looked like anyone—but I really wasn't paying that much attention, because I wanted to get the van."

That's what I was afraid of. Now he could be anyone. He could be strolling around town wearing big sunglasses, maybe talking in a funny accent like a foreign movie star, or he could be selling used cars, or even delivering pizza to our front door. He could become an Amish farmer with an Amish wife and kids, but even if he was driving a horse and buggy and clip-clopping down the road he'd still have that Pigza head full of nonsense and he'd be shifting about in his seat just waiting to cut loose and make a run for the winner's circle. But he'll just be going in circles until he figures out how to be comfortable in his own skin—not some borrowed skin but the skin he was born in.

Suddenly the dogs were tired of me not paying attention to them. They tugged on their leashes and bounced up and down like springs. I knelt down and scratched their backs. "Look," I said to El Gordo, holding him by his chin as he growled up at me. "This is a name change announcement. You are no longer El Gordo and she is no longer Quesadilla. From now on you are plain old Pablo Pigza and she is Pablita Pigza and I'd appreciate it when you bark at me if you are thinking, 'Joey! Joey! Joey!' Fred is dead. You got it?"

I stood and leaned against a car for a minute because I still got light-headed when I bent over.

I couldn't take the dogs inside the hospital so I tied them to the smokers' bench out front where Dad had picked those smoky flowers for me. "No eating cigarette butts," I ordered. "Bite anyone who tries to take you, and I'll be back as soon as I can."

I went into the gift shop. I didn't have any money to buy something fancy but it didn't matter to me. Money never really changed our lives anyway. We had a second chance but we let it fall through a hole in our pockets. It wasn't about the money. It was us. It was like we were the big hole and anything put into us fell out. I picked out a card with a photograph on the front of a baby dressed as a bee wrapped in a blanket. I took it up to the counter.

"Can I pay you back in a little while?" I asked the lady, and gave her my best smile. "I promise."

"Sure," she said.

I borrowed her pen and drew a big heart inside the card. That was Mom's heart. Inside that heart I drew another. That was mine. Inside of that one I drew another. That was the baby's. Then down at the bottom of Mom's big heart I drew two little ones, for Pablo and Pablita. They were our family, too.

When I got back up to Mom's floor I was feeling a

little better. I had the card but, more than that, I had my own good name. I stood at Mom's open door and looked in after her.

"I bet he's gone, isn't he?" she said, looking back across the room at me.

"I don't know," I said, and stood by her side with the card. "I can't tell for sure."

"Well, I can," she said. "Once the money was gone he was itchin' to bolt."

That's when I remembered to tell her about Dad crying when he was looking at the baby.

"That makes sense," she snapped. "He always cries just before he runs off. It's his signature emotion before he heads for the hills. Plus this." She held out a sheet of paper.

"What is it?"

"The nurse brought it in," she said.

I took it from her hand. It was a birth certificate that Dad had filled out and signed. For the baby's name he had written: Junior Carter Pigza.

"I guess the Heinz family has officially vanished," I announced.

"Like a Heinz genie gone back into the ketchup bottle," she said, and laughed at her own joke.

"Well, that leaves me the oldest boy, so I'm the *big man* in charge again," I claimed. I pointed to her and made my first family announcement. "You are Fran Pigza," I said. "The baby will be called Junior Pigza, and you know me—I'm Joey Pigza!" It felt good to say my name so I said it again, only louder. "I'm Joey Pigza!"

"I'll be counting on you," she said.

"Do you think it is just too easy to be something you are not?" I asked, thinking of Dad.

"Easy in the beginning," she said. "But after a while even the made-up self starts to gather baggage, and before you know it you might just as well have stayed your old self."

"I was tired of Freddy," I said.

"Maria was getting on my nerves," she added. "Kind of like a guest who wouldn't leave."

"She shopped a lot," I remarked.

"Yeah," she said. "But you know why I was doing it all the time?"

" 'Cause you wanted to buy stuff," I guessed.

"I saw this coming from a long way off," she said. "If some part of me didn't love him a lot I'd never see his weak side. They say love is blind, but for me it's the opposite. It makes me see the good in him, too, which is why I can never hate him."

"I just learned that," I said. "Once I forgave him I couldn't get mad at him anymore."

"You and I think alike," she said.

"So then why'd you get back together with him?"

"Hope," she said without regret. "I had hope that he had changed for the better. And for a while it was promising. But I don't regret it—we have Junior."

"Yeah," I said. "I love being a brother."

"He is *muy magnífico*," she sighed, "but I think he is going to be worse than you. Did you notice that he has a cowlick in the front of his head and in the back? That means he'll be coming and going at the same time."

The thought of a cow licking him made me laugh. "We can't screw this one up," I said. "He's the Pigza of the future."

"He's that and more," she murmured.

"Is it strange having a kid?" I asked.

"Yeah, it's like marrying someone you never met."

"Better that than remarrying someone you have met," I said.

"Yes," she said, and laughed, then quickly looked away as her hands covered her face. I think she was crying, but whatever she was feeling she wanted to keep private.

"I better go check on the dogs," I said as I stood up and walked toward the door. "I don't want them to think the rest of us have run off." Then, in case she was crying, I added, "I'll be back."

A NOTE FROM THE AUTHOR

When I was a boy, all my favorite friends were like Joey Pigza. They were wild, out of control, fun, smart, and slightly insane. For instance, my good friend Frankie Pagoda was a genius at thinking up dangerous activities nobody should ever try. He had a swimming pool in his backyard and every day he would climb a ladder and get on top of his roof then run down the slope of the roof and dive into his swimming pool. That bored him after a while, so he hauled his bicycle up to the top of the roof and rode it down—but he missed the pool. He flew through the air and hit his head on the concrete edge of the pool, and I thought he had killed himself, but despite the huge dent in his head, he was OK. He also invented the "Ring of Fire"—a game where we would roller skate down a metal slide and dive headfirst through a burning hula hoop that had been soaked in kerosene. That was good.

Then there was my old friend Kenny Diehl who invited me into his basement, where he kept a live, six-foot-long alligator as a pet. We would play a game called "Alligator Wrestler" …

So when I grew up, I knew a lot of kids as wild as Joey Pigza, and I loved them. But my family moved a lot, and I ended up going to ten different schools in twelve grades, so all my friends disappeared into my past. Also, as I moved on in my life, without the influence of my wild friends I became a quiet reader and a writer.

But one day, my wild old past was suddenly reawakened. I was speaking to students at a school. There was a wiry kid in the front row who was a little bit jittery. As I spoke, he was spinning in circles at his desk. But he was clearly very smart because as soon as I would start a sentence he would cut me off by blurting out exactly what I was about to say. I would start a sentence and he would finish it. He really seemed to like this game as he spun around and around in his seat, but then suddenly something changed for him. He kept waving his arm to gain the teacher's attention, but she was busy with another student. Finally, the spinning boy could not hold back what he needed to say any longer and he hollered out, "Teacher! Teacher! I forgot to take my meds!" She just pointed to the classroom door and he shot out of his desk and through the door. I heard him running down the hallway to the nurse's office, punching all the metal lockers, which went "Bam! Bam! Bam!" about a hundred times in a row.

At that moment, I knew he was a great kid. That night as I sat down to write in my journal, I remembered that kid and wrote about him. And then I remembered my old friends—Frankie, Kenny, and others. It was at that moment I began to write the first Joey Pigza book—and in a way Joey has now become another of my wild old friends.

GOFISH

Jack Gantos

What did you want to be when you grew up?
I didn't have much sense of myself as a future adult with a job when I was a child. I'm sure I projected somewhat into my future but was probably happier thinking I would remain a child. I did pass through many stages along the way to being a writer—an anthropologist and archaeologist were the two most attractive.

When did you realize you wanted to be a writer?
In high school, it suddenly occurred to me that most adults I knew were fairly miserable because they were stuck in jobs they did not like. So I made a list of things I liked to do and reading and writing and bookish things were at the top of my list. I liked books. Writing was a constant challenge. I knew I would never be bored with it.

What's your first childhood memory?
It is either burying my plastic buffalo in my grandmother's back-yard, or lighting matches in my uncle's closet.

What's your most embarrassing childhood memory?
Eating too many hot peppers one night, which was followed the next day with an ill-timed public bowel explosion. Either this, or the time my sister locked me naked out of the house, and the lady next door caught me as I tried to borrow some of her female attire off the clothesline in order to hide my shameful nakedness. I could go on, but I think these two examples are sufficient.

As a young person, who did you look up to most?
I loved the old explorers. I wanted to be Captain Cook. I used to act out his death in my front yard.

What was your worst subject in school?
Algebra.

What was your first job?
Bag boy at Winn-Dixie grocery store in Fort Lauderdale, Florida. I was fourteen. They paid $1.20 per hour. I loved that job. That is when I learned that money was power.

How did you celebrate publishing your first book?
I did a little happy dance in the middle of Park Street in Boston—where I had just sold the book to Houghton Mifflin. I've walked by that spot thousands of times on my way to the library. It still makes me smile.

Where do you write your books?
The library. Almost all my books are written in libraries.

Where do you find inspiration for your writing?
I pay close attention to my life. I read a lot. I travel. I talk to people.

Which of your characters is most like you?
Jack Henry, from the Jack Henry series. He is me. Also I wrote a memoir, *Hole in My Life*, and that is most certainly me. And in *Dead End in Norvelt*, a good bit of my DNA is in that book.

When you finish a book, who reads it first?
Usually my editor. I don't share manuscripts too often. I don't belong to a writer's group or any of that sort of thing. It's very helpful for me to make my own mistakes.

Are you a morning person or a night owl?
Morning person.

What's your idea of the best meal ever?
Sushi on the docks in Tokyo. Wild boar in Bangkok. Green curry in Singapore. Peking duck in Beijing. (I could go on.)

Which do you like better: cats or dogs?
Cats. I have two.

What do you value most in your friends?
Their patience with me. I'm an odd friend. I'm not quite an Edward Gorey character, but almost.

Where do you go for peace and quiet?
The library.

What makes you laugh out loud?
A clever character in a book. A snippet of dialog that is so sharp, so delicious, so funny that you wish you had thought of it.

What's your favorite song?
The Rolling Stones: "Satisfaction."

Who is your favorite fictional character?
Tough question. Gregor Samsa was the first to come to mind so he wins the race. Ishmael in *Moby-Dick* is pretty darn good, too. I love Adrian Mole, Harry from *Harry the Dirty Dog*, Holden Caulfield, Winston Smith . . . And the list goes on and on, oh, and don't forget Eloise, Piper Paw . . . There are just too many.

What are you most afraid of?
That somehow my weakest qualities are going to result in letting other people down.

What time of the year do you like best?
The fall is always the best. It is the most complicated season. I find the fear of death is far more powerful than the desire to create life. Plus, fall smells better.

What is your favorite TV show?
My favorite show was always *The Avengers*. These days I like watching surgical procedures on TV.

If you were stranded on a desert island, who would you want for company?
Certainly not Robinson Crusoe. I'll go with Superman. Someone who can get me off the island. If Captain Jack Sparrow can get me off the island, then I would prefer him.

If you could travel in time, where would you go?
The sacking of Rome. The last stone set in the great pyramid at Giza. I could skip the burning of the great library at Alexandria. That would kill me. Also, I always wish I could go back in time and help the Neanderthal people out. I wonder what books they might have written. Also, I wouldn't mind having season tickets to the Globe Theatre in London when Shakespeare was putting on his cycle of Histories.

What's the best advice you have ever received about writing?
Read good books. Keep a journal. Write every day. Trust yourself. Take advantage of every good thought. Laziness will kill your dreams with a self-inflicted wound.

What do you want readers to remember about your books?
I want the reader to remember how they felt the day after reading one of my books. My book will remain the same. But I always wonder how the reader has been transformed.

What would you do if you ever stopped writing?
I don't honestly know. I suppose I would return to being a college professor. I did that for eighteen years and liked it well enough. I suspect, however, that I'd end up doing something completely different—like being a long-haul trucker—something with a lot of solitude.

What do you like best about yourself?
That's a short list.
I don't like to give up.

JOEY PIGZA FAN MAIL

Dear Jack Gantos,

When Joey loses control, he is exactly like me when I don't take my medicine . . . Sometimes I do lose control even when I take my medication because I get angry for doing things wrong . . . Sometimes I wish I was normal like my brother and my sister or my other classmates . . . The book made me feel that there are other people in the world like me. It's not just me who acts like that. The book helped me understand myself better. It tells me what Joey does with his problems . . . The only difference is the way we behave and the way we do things to help us. He listens to a tape player and I just go to my room and draw my favorite things. That is how Joey is exactly like me.

Dear Mr. Gantos,

I would like to tell you how much I'm like Joey. For instance, I have a trumpet, I've never seen my dad before, I have the same problems as Joey but not as bad, I have a dog, my mom works at a beauty parlor, we lived with my grandma for a little bit, and I also get into trouble a little too much . . .

   P.S. My favorite part was when Joey covered himself with shaving cream!

Dear Mr. Jack Gantos,

People usually need to see how bad someone else has it before they recognize how good they have it. This book has made me see

What is your worst habit?
Whining.

What do you consider to be your greatest accomplishment?
My family.

What do you wish you could do better?
Lie.

What would your readers be most surprised to learn about you?
I lie to myself more than I lie to others.

When I had breakfast at the White House, I did not steal any of the silverware because I thought that if I become president it would be like stealing from myself.

Perhaps they would be most surprised to learn about my prison record in *Hole in My Life*.

what a great life I have. I would recommend *Joey Pigza Swallowed the Key* to anyone who thinks "the grass is always greener on the other side of the fence"! Thank you for making me appreciate myself, my family, and my life!

Jack Gantos,

Good job! I really like that Joey Pigza book you wrote . . . Can you give me something of yours? Please not a piece of your trash.

Dear Jack Gantos,

I'm doing a project on you because you inspire me. I also have ADHD just like you did when you were little. What grade did you find out that you had ADHD? I found out in fourth grade. I read all of the Joey Pigza books . . . You are my favorite author.

P.S. I also wear the med patches like Joey Pigza.

Dear Mr. Gantos,

I have ADHD. I take meds like Joey and they usually wear off at lunchtime (ha, ha). That's when my teachers call me wired. When I was in third grade I wasn't on the meds I'm on now and I was placed in a school like Joey was in the book. I was in that school for four years. That's a lot of years to be in a school like that. Like Joey Pigza I was sent back to my old school. It was real hard coming back and having regular classes all day long . . . As a class we listened to Joey Pigza and every time he did something funny I laughed because I thought of me and what I did in the classrooms. This is the best book I ever read because it is just like my life and what I went through.

Dear Mr. Gantos,

When you walk outside do people know you're a famous author? My best part in *Joey Pigza Loses Control* is when Joey Pigza shoots a peanut out of his nose. I tried that.

    P.S. You're the best author.

Dear Mr. Gantos,

I'm a huge fan of your book *Joey Pigza Swallowed the Key*. I love that your book is sad and funny ... We read it as a class so if I wanted to read ahead I couldn't ... If you want to know more about me, can I get back to you on that?

Dear Mr. Gantos,

I love your book ... because you explain a lot and you paint pictures in my head.

Dear Mr. Gantos,

I love your books. Have you ever made Joey a spy? ... I can't wait when the fifth book might come out and it could be *Joey the Spy!*

Joey is certain he can pull his family together—
if only his family doesn't pull him apart first.
Keep reading for a sneak peek at Joey's
next misadventure!

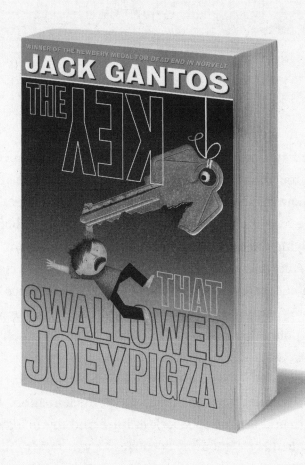

THE ORACLE

Like I said, when I'm just a little bit of trouble people give me extra help because they think they can teach me how to help myself, which is always their hope, and mine too. Today my new teacher, Mrs. Fabian, had us studying ancient Greek mythology by acting it out.

"This year we'll live like the Greeks!" she declared with enthusiasm, and pointed to a map of Greece and a list of names and places she had tacked to the wall. She pointed out Mount Olympus, where all the gods and goddesses lived, and the dark underworld called Hades, and told us great stories about the Minotaur and Hercules and so much more ancient life. "We'll eat, drink, and sleep Greek culture and mythology!"

I liked her right away because she was talking about having fun *before* we went over the list of class rules.

Still, there was something bothering me that I needed to ask her, so I raised my hand.

"Yes, Joey?" she asked.

"Are we going to be tested on that?"

"Not yet," she replied, and smiled widely. "We're going to enjoy learning it first."

"After we enjoy it," I asked, "then will we be tested?"

"We'll see," she said.

"See a test?" I shot back.

"You are a clever boy," she replied, trying to put the brakes on me. "Don't stress out. Always remember that the more fun you have the better you'll do on a test."

"But all my life I've been tested and I do stress out a little bit," I said with my heart pounding inside my chest like a fist punching its way out. "Because right now I'm repeating a whole year, which means I totally failed *everything* on last year's test. You name it and I flunked it!"

By then I had everyone's attention so I tried to be helpful and blurted, "Testing turns me into a stress-mess. Everyone else, too!"

"Well, in that case," Mrs. Fabian swiftly cut in, "you need a fun job that can bring out the best-mess in you." She snapped her fingers and right then and there gave me the job in class everyone else wanted. I became the Greek Oracle at Delphi and wore a Greek toga around my shoulders as I sat at her desk, and everyone lined up in front of me like troubled ancient Greeks with big problems. Instead of *me* being worried, it was their job to look worried, and then one by one they were to whisper their questions in my ear. My job was to listen, then "Greekishly" slap my palm up against my forehead, and roll my eyes inward, and moan like a ghostly wind, and then come up with a prediction. I liked this job because everyone always said I was a natural at being dramatic.

My first anguished Greek was Henry Darts. "O Oracle," he chanted in a wavering voice that Mrs. Fabian had first acted out. "What do you see in my future?"

He didn't give me much to work with, plus he was my first troubled Greek and I hadn't practiced my oracling yet. I have always been better at asking questions than at giving answers, so I hesitated as I twisted up my face into a question mark and scratched the side of my peanut head like a thinking monkey. Then suddenly I flicked my eyes open and in a whispery voice I told Chuck I had a vision of him on an ambulance stretcher after school. "You will stick your left hand into a baseball glove . . . and a black widow spider will bite you . . . and your hand will swell up so big not even Hercules can pull the glove off," I added dramatically.

"Do I survive?" he asked with his voice fading away

like someone falling off a cliff. He gaped at his hand in horror.

"Watch the TV news tonight," I replied in my moaning, windy voice. "If you are not dead, then the Greek gods have spared you."

I thought I did well, but he must have run off crying to Mrs. Fabian because she soon snuck up on me from behind and dropped her arms crossways over my chest like a seat belt, and then she tightened them.

"Remember," she said softly into my ear, "your job is to make sure everyone has a good day."

She lifted her arms and I took a breath.

"Well," I said, looking straight up at her, "when am *I* going to have a good day?" It wasn't that I was having a bad day, but if I had a chance to talk to a real oracle I'd want some answers about my missing meds, and how Mom was going to take care of Carter Junior and the dogs while I was at school.

"Well?" I repeated.

"Not every question gets an answer," Mrs. Fabian replied as if she was the boss oracle.

"Why?" I asked. "What goes *up* must come *down*, so it figures that every question has an answer."

"Not in this case," she explained. "Some questions go up, up, and away—*poof!*" She snapped her fingers above my head.

"That sounds so negative," I remarked, trying to stay a step ahead of her.

"It's negative to waste your time thinking up questions that don't have answers yet. Relax," she advised.

I knew she was right, because my brain was built as upside down as an iceberg. All my millions of questions were gathered on the bottom of my brain and I only had a few little answers melting across the top.

"But," she said cheerfully, steering right around my negative thoughts, "when you are *positive*, then every day is a good day. Now, can I make a prediction just for you?" Mrs. Fabian asked.

"Go ahead," I said. "Peek into my future—but watch out you don't get poked in the eye."

She held one hand over her eyes and rubbed her forehead. Then she leaned down and calmly said, "The key for you to have a sunny day is when you unlock all the good in the world, and not all the bad."

"Is there a keyhole I can peek into and see all that good stuff that's waiting for me?" I asked. "I don't want to unlock any more bad stuff."

"Just be positive," she instructed, "and even the bad stuff will turn into good stuff." Then she glanced up at the clock because someone had to go down to the cafeteria and get the classroom snack.

"Pos-i-tive," I said, cutting the word into slices like a pizza.

"Now say it with the appropriate feeling," she said, and encouraged me to brighten up my tone by making a face as perky as a sunflower.

"*Pawz-i-tive,*" I said softly, like I was gently petting Carter Junior's head. "*Pawz-i-tive,*" I repeated, until after a few tries I made that word sound like it had an optimistic future. "I'm *pawzzz-i-tive,*" I said to Mrs. Fabian, and licked my lips because all those *zzz*'s tickled them.

"And I'm *positive* you are," she replied. "Now be a ray of sunshine. Remember, your good day reward will be waiting for you once you make everyone feel less *negative.*"

Secretly I knew she really stressed the word *positive* because of my past, and even though she didn't know a whole lot about my present, I could tell that someone had filled her in on me before I even walked through her door. I bet she had a file on me titled: JOEY PIGZA: *TOP SECRET!*

I told the next kid there was a dollar in lost change behind his couch cushions. That was positive.

"O Great Oracle," a girl named Shirley asked, bowing toward me as she spoke, "what will my mother cook for dinner?"

"What's your favorite food?" I moaned.

"Chicken under a brick," she replied.

"That's exactly what she is cooking," I said, sounding a little astonished. In a million years I couldn't have guessed that people would eat a poor chicken after they flattened it with a brick.

The next kid was missing his turtle and I said he'd find it in his bedroom slipper—his left one. Another kid wanted to know what was for her birthday. I told her the answer would show up in her wildest dreams just before her alarm clock went off.

By the time I finished with the whole class I was pretty good at being positive. The other kids even smiled at me as if I had been handing out candy. As a result I sat up smartly in my seat and tilted my head back. I closed my eyes. Now it was my turn to ask the Greek gods a question and receive my own special answer. I took a deep breath. "When will my mother feel better?" I dared to ask.

At that moment a stuttering, scratchy intercom voice came on over the classroom loudspeaker.

"Mrs. Fabian," the sandpaper voice said. "Can you hear me?"

"Yes," Mrs. Fabian replied loudly, glancing up at the speaker. So we all glanced up at the speaker, which at that moment looked like a round-faced oracle from Mount Olympus about to tell us something important.

As we waited for the office voice to return we heard some switches clicking back and forth, and then a worried, desperate voice came snaking through the speaker. "Only Joey can help me," the voice said in a whispery way. "Only Joey."

Everyone in class suddenly turned and looked at me. "Who was that?" asked a wide-eyed kid.

"A Greek goddess?" someone guessed.

But it wasn't a god or goddess. It was my mother. But how could it be her? I must have been hearing voices. I shot a puzzled look at Mrs. Fabian, and she was staring right back at me.

Then the switches clicked back the other way and the secretary's voice returned. "Sorry about that," she said breathlessly, and quickly added, "Send Joey Pigza down to the office—*immediately!*" I knew it! Someone must have asked that radio oracle to name the first kid to get in trouble on the first day of school.

But why would the oracle sound like my mother?

Mrs. Fabian turned her eyes toward the door. Her nose was like a needle on a compass and I slowly sailed away. "Are they going to test me on something I know?" I asked over my shoulder, hoping they would test me on changing diapers and cleaning up baby puke because I'd done a lot of that this last while.

"I think they are just going to fill you in on something you don't yet know," she said. "Don't worry. Skip on down there with your sunflower face held high. I predict it will be good news."

I didn't have to be an oracle to know it wasn't good news and the only thing that skipped down the hall was my heart skipping a beat.

READ ALL THE JOEY PIGZA BOOKS!

JOEY PIGZA SWALLOWED THE KEY
National Book Award Finalist

978-1-250-06168-3

JOEY PIGZA LOSES CONTROL
Newbery Honor Book

978-1-250-06167-6

WHAT WOULD JOEY DO?

978-1-250-06169-0

I AM NOT JOEY PIGZA

978-1-250-06166-9

THE KEY THAT SWALLOWED JOEY PIGZA

978-0-374-30083-8

mackids.com